The Green Shade

ROBIN MAUGHAM

The Green Shade

HEINEMANN : LONDON

William Heinemann Ltd
LONDON MELBOURNE TORONTO
CAPE TOWN AUCKLAND

First published 1966
Reprinted 1966
© Robin Maugham, 1966

Printed in Great Britain by
Cox & Wyman Ltd., London, Fakenham and Reading

For Peter

'There's darkness and rats now in the Garden of Eden . . . But I'm certain of this . . . To understand is to love.'

PART ONE

1

H E awoke as the studio Humber drew up outside the house in Upper Grosvenor Street. The driver held open the car door for him.

'Same time tomorrow morning?'

'No, thanks,' Graham said. 'I'll be away for a few days. I'll call the studio when I get back.'

'New project, Mr Hadley?'

'Could be – with any luck. Good night, and thanks.'

The old house had recently been converted into flats, and the hall with its thick leather-upholstered sofas and heavy blue curtains reminded him of an opulent padded cell. As he moved towards the lift he caught a glimpse of himself in a mirror. He was forty-five years old, and for once he looked it. The hall-porter was watching him contemptuously. This pert stare had embarrassed Graham at first, but he had stopped worrying when he had discovered that all the tenants were given the same treatment when they looked at themselves in the glass.

'Good evening,' he called out.

''Vninsir,' the porter mumbled.

This dialogue only varied at Christmas when Graham slid a five-pound note into his hand.

Graham took the lift to the third floor. The long day's work had exhausted him so much that it was an effort to search for his keys and let himself into his flat. He walked into his living-room and poured himself a whisky-and-soda. Lying on the marble-topped table beside the piano was a slip of paper on which there was scrawled a message.

3

'A Mrs Millington phoned.

You've run out of tonic water so I've paid for it from the money I found on your dressing-table.

Yours truly, Mrs Lucas.'

The telephone rang and he took up the receiver.

'How did it go today?'

Cole Edwards always presumed that his soft precise voice with its faint American accent would be recognized, and he was usually right. He was one of the highest-paid script-writers in England, and Graham had put him under contract for his next film.

'Are you worn to a frazzle?'

'Practically,' Graham said. 'Cutting's always the worst part, I find.'

'Have you got a drink?'

'What do you suppose?'

'Then take a great swig and I'll tell you the worst. Mae Millington's expecting you to turn up at her party tonight, and you can't get out of it.'

'Can't you tell her that I've gone to Paris?'

'She knows you're not going until tomorrow morning. You *must* go, Graham. Besides, Cy Lancaster will be there and he might do us some good.'

'I doubt it. I only met him once but he struck me as phoney, and location pictures don't interest him. Anyhow, he probably thinks Abdel Krim is the name of a Moroccan night-club. . . . Are you going?'

'I haven't been asked, thank heavens. But I honestly don't see how you can get out of it.'

'Damn!'

'I'll ring you first thing in the morning to let you know what plane we're on. My dizzy secretary has made a slight muddle of our reservations. Any old how, enjoy yourself.

4

Graham put down the receiver and decided to give himself another drink before he shaved and had a shower. In the old days – an unknown young man from Birmingham – he would have welcomed an invitation to Mae's house. He always seemed to get what he wanted in life too late, he reflected, and if he continued to drink so heavily it would be too late for love – should that miracle occur a second time.

He kept his Bentley in a mews garage round the corner from his flat; he used the studio car to drive to his work so that he could relax or read letters or a script during the hour's drive there and back. To own a Bentley had once seemed a goal, but now it was only another milestone he had passed on the road of his success.

Light May rain was falling; the pavement was gleaming outside the white façade of Mae's house in Chelsea Square, which was lined on all sides with cars. Graham found a place to park and walked through the open door of the brightly-lit house, nodded good evening to the ascetic-looking butler, and climbed up the left-hand flight of the branching staircase. Mae Millington was a tall, stocky woman of about fifty with firmly muscled legs. She advanced across her green-and-gilt drawing-room in precisely the same way as she strode with her pack of beagles across the Sussex downs. With her wealth and her passion for celebrities in show business, she was, he decided, the whipper-in of café society. As she embraced him extravagantly and kissed him on both cheeks he felt the pins concealed in her hair against his skin.

'Darling,' she said in her deep hoarse voice. '*Mille mille grazie* for the tickets for your preview.'

5

'I only hope you'll enjoy it,' he replied, smiling automatically.

While she talked, his eyes wandered round the room. Most of her usual group was there – an American film star, who had flown over on an expense account to watch his horse run at Newmarket, an English novelist whose fame rested on a best-seller of a decade ago, Lady Julia Grant whose face had been lifted so often that her gigolos said her skin was stretched so tight that she couldn't close her eyes and her mouth at the same time, two or three B-picture film-producers, Elizabeth Sayers – an unsuccessful film-actress of twenty-five who had been his mistress for three hectic months a year ago – and the inevitable sprinkling of young men in tight blue suits and stiff white collars who wrote for the gossip columns. Graham's gaze panned, like a camera, slowly round them and then stopped suddenly. The young girl in the plain black dress who was standing by the tapestry quite close to him had long fair hair and a face that with its fine bone formation had been constructed to last. But it was her eyes which held him. She had the odd look of a child who has been unexpectedly hurt. She was staring back at him steadily, and for a moment he felt that some important communication was being made by their eyes as if they were transmitting sets exchanging urgent messages in code. It seemed a long time before she looked away.

Mae seized two glasses of whisky from a waiter's tray, poured them into a large Lalique tumbler that she found on a side-table, and handed the drink to Graham.

'From one alcoholic to another,' she giggled.

While Mae talked, Graham watched the girl, hoping to catch her eye again. She was about eighteen years old and very slender. Apart from two gold bracelets on her wrist she wore no jewellery. A well-built husky young man with untidy black hair was standing beside her; Graham saw him put his arm possessively on her shoulder and then whisper something to her. The girl raised her head and smiled at him like a conspirator and laughed. For a moment Graham was glad that he was a detached onlooker, in no way involved. Mae was eating a chicken *vol-au-vent*.

'Who's that girl in black standing by the tapestry?' he asked.

Mae briskly swallowed a large piece of pastry.

'Her name's Vicky something-or-other. My godson brought her. He's the handsome young man standing next to the girl.'

The food seemed to have made her voice deeper. She took his hand firmly and led him across the room.

'Simon and Vicky,' she said, 'I want you to meet Graham Hadley.'

Graham watched the girl intently and waited for her eyes to meet his.

'Hullo,' she said, smiling at him.

Now that he was close to her he was disarmed by the combination of delicacy and arrogance in her face, which was made unusual by her sad, beautiful eyes. They were soft and insecure. He found himself almost afraid to study her features closely for fear that her face might lose its magic. As her companion held out his hand Graham sensed hostility.

'We've met before,' the young man said.

Graham looked at him blankly.

'I auditioned for *The Strawberry Patch*.'

Graham tried to remember the face. He was now certain he had seen it before. Perhaps the young man had been a stand-in.

'I hope you were successful,' Graham said pleasantly.

'No, I wasn't.' The voice was hard and flat. Graham's

eyes darted towards Vicky. She was watching them both carefully. Graham realized that his only chance depended on his next move. He brought from his pocket a thin gold-edged wallet and took out a card.

'Next time you see in the trade papers that I'm making a film, do give me a ring and I'll see what I can do.'

'Thanks.'

Graham took this opportunity to turn to Vicky.

'Did you see that film?' he asked.

'Yes.'

'What did you think of it?'

'I thought the book was much better.'

Graham laughed.

'So did the author,' he said. 'They usually do.'

'Graham!'

He turned to find his hostess behind him. Mae was still hard at work. She had herded a middle-aged couple towards them.

'Graham, you do know Cherry and Cy Lancaster,' she said. 'Cy flew in from Hollywood last week to produce a television series.'

Graham greeted the Americans with sufficient familiarity to seem friendly should they have remembered meeting him before and enough formality to appear polite if they hadn't. Cy Lancaster's pale bald head and large ears were made all the more unusual by his height and his carefully preserved figure. Graham could imagine him on the bathroom floor straining at his daily press-ups. Evidently he had chosen his wife to provide a contrast. She was almost half his height and twice his width with faded blonde hair and a snub nose. Defiantly she wore an uplift brassière.

'Mr Hadley,' she sighed, 'I just have to tell you that Cy and me saw your film in New York, and let me say that we left the theatre on a seventh cloud. Now you must tell me. What was in the back of your mind when you made that poor man take those pills?'

Graham looked at her earnestly, then smiled. 'To be frank,' he said, 'a woman with your kind of charm.'

Cherry Lancaster took a deep breath. 'That's the nicest thing anybody's said to me for a long time,' she said, turning to her husband for approval. But Graham could see that Cy wasn't quite sure about the remark, for he moved away.

Graham glanced at Vicky, whose face had wrinkled mischievously. He winked at her, elated to have made some contact at last, and he was about to speak to her when he felt an arm around his shoulder. Beside him stood a squat, red-faced man of sixty. His name was Tarrisch, and he owned a film studio near Henley.

'I thought you were in Paris, my boy,' Tarrisch said in his booming mid-European voice.

Vicky turned away to Simon, and Graham resigned himself to a short conversation.

'I leave tomorrow morning,' he said.

While they talked, Graham finished his drink and took another glass from the waiter who was passing. Tarrisch was asking him some question.

'How's the latest film doing?'

'As well as can be expected.'

Tarrisch patted Graham's back affectionately with a plump white hand.

'Remember that any time you want to change your studio my offer's still open.'

Graham knew that he was trying to sell his studio and move to Madrid.

'Thanks,' he replied. 'I won't forget.'

As he spoke, Cherry Lancaster hurried over to him.

9

'You must join in Cy's game,' she panted. 'It's really fascinating. You'll be simply amazed how much you find out about people. It's so revealing it's almost scarifying.'

She took his arm and pulled him towards her husband who was sitting on the floor like a Red Indian chief in an early Western, surrounded by a group of surprised but polite faces. His ears were twitching with the effort to assert himself.

'Are we all ready?' he called out loudly. Then he pointed a well-manicured finger-nail at Graham. 'You must join in,' he stated.

'All right,' Graham replied.

'And you must come next.'

'Very well.'

'Now, sir,' Cy Lancaster said in a voice of authority, 'if you were a garden, what kind of garden would you be?'

Graham thought for a moment. He had played the game before. 'If I were a garden, I'd be a long sweeping lawn. I'd have very few flowers, perhaps a few rose beds, and an ornamental fountain – probably by Bernini.'

Cy listened with an absurd intensity, and Graham controlled a desire to laugh.

'Would your garden have a wall?' Cy demanded earnestly.

'A very high wall,' Graham replied in the same tone of voice.

'And if you were a bottle, what kind of bottle would you be?'

'I'd be one of those big Armagnac bottles,' Graham replied immediately. 'The kind you see at the end of bars.'

'And if you were a key?'

'A dungeon key.'

Cherry Lancaster giggled nervously. Her husband frowned at her.

10

'And would your key fit into your bottle?' The question was asked with such reverence that Graham allowed himself to smile for the first time.

'I'm afraid not,' he answered.

Cy turned thoughtfully to face Vicky.

'Now then,' he said, 'let's have a line on your garden.'

Vicky stretched out for a cigarette and lit it from the lighter on the table beside her.

'My garden would run down to a brook,' she said. 'There would be a country lane that runs along one side of it, and on that side there'd be a wall.'

'Would it be a very high wall?' Cy asked.

'No,' Vicky replied. 'High enough to stop people looking over it, but low enough to allow those who really tried. It would be a wall covered with wild roses. There is a lawn, but it needs mowing, and it's strewn with buttercups and dandelions. And all around the garden there's a rather untidy herbaceous border.'

Cy nodded his head appreciatively.

'And if you were a bottle?' he asked.

'Oh, I'd be a hock bottle.'

'And if you were a key?'

'A car key.'

'And would your key fit into your bottle?'

Vicky was silent. She had covered her right eye with her hand. Cy waited tensely for her answer. Suddenly Vicky stood up, and as she moved Graham noticed that she had tears in her eyes.

'It would just fit,' she said vaguely. Then she walked quickly out of the room.

Tarrisch shifted his position and unfolded his legs.

'What's the point of the game anyway?' he demanded.

Cy turned to him. 'It's of enormous psychological importance,' he said.

'How so?' Tarrisch asked.

'Well – to take a simple example – if a person's key doesn't fit into his or her bottle it shows that subconsciously he or she is dominantly masculine; if it does fit, then the person is dominantly feminine.'

'In the case of your last two victims,' said Tarrisch, 'I wouldn't have thought there was much doubt.'

'You can never be certain,' Cherry Lancaster said. 'I knew a full general in the British army with hair all over his chest, and he said that his key would fit into his bottle as easily as a pickle into a jam-jar.'

Graham got up, helped himself to a drink, and moved towards the door in search of Vicky. He found her standing at the far end of the hall in front of a long mirror. Her face was contorted and she was pulling down her lower eyelid.

'Have you got something in your eye?' Graham asked.

She did not turn from the mirror. Her hands fell sharply to her side.

'I've lost a contact lens,' she said.

'Has it fallen out?'

Her face was taut. She seemed to resent his interest. Graham had once received the same cold stare when releasing his secretary who had locked herself in the lavatory by mistake. Vicky now began to fish into the corner of her eye with her first and second fingers.

'So the lens is still in?'

'It's one of the small kind that just covers the iris,' she said in a dull voice.

Graham watched the tears streaming down her cheeks as she became exasperated. Then the lens slipped back into position, and she gave a sigh and began to make up her face.

'Isn't it desperately uncomfortable when the lens slips out of place?'

12

'You get used to it,' she said.

Graham took a sip of his drink.

'Why are you so determined not to like me?' he asked quietly.

Vicky blinked several times at the mirror. 'I'm not,' she said.

Graham put down his drink on a table beside him.

'Then won't you look at me?'

She turned and leaned against the Empire side-table on which Graham had put his glass. She looked at him wryly, and he realized that she thought he was drunk.

'I'm a little tired,' he said, 'but I'm not high, and there's something I must tell you. . . . When I first saw you this evening and our eyes met across the room, I had a strong feeling that in some kind of way there was a communication between us. You must have felt something too . . . because you looked at me for quite a time as well.'

He watched her face for some reaction, but there was none.

'I'm sometimes psychic,' he said. 'And I know. I know that you're what I've been trying to find for a very long time.'

She smiled. 'How long?'

'Let's say for a dozen years.'

He glanced down at his glass of whisky beside her. It was half-full, and he longed to finish it, but he did not want her to think that what he said to her was influenced by alcohol.

'Please don't think that this is a standard line,' he continued. 'I mean every word of it . . . The fact that I'm not completely sober makes me all the more certain of my instinct. . . I must talk to you. Really I must. . . . When this finishes, will you come back to my flat? I promise I won't lay a finger on you.'

'Are you mad?'

13

Graham looked surprised, and she laughed, but it was not an unpleasant laugh.

'Look,' she said, 'you're very sweet. But I met you about half an hour ago, and I'm not living by my wits.'

He winced. 'If you don't like the idea of my flat, then let's go to a bar,' he said. 'Let's go anywhere you fancy. But it must be tonight. I'm leaving for Paris tomorrow.'

'It's still impossible. My boy friend's waiting for me in the next room.'

'And you won't come?'

'Don't be silly. I can't possibly come.'

He moved his glass farther on to the table.

'Well, at least will you give me your telephone number?'

She opened her handbag and took out a card.

'Have you got something to write with?'

He handed her his pen and was amazed at the speed with which she wrote. He read the card on which was printed in plain type the words Vicky Tollard. Below she had added an address in Earl's Court and a telephone number.

'Thanks,' he said. 'I'll ring you tomorrow before I leave.'

She stood up and handed him his drink.

'You'll wonder where you got that card when you find it in your pocket tomorrow morning,' she said.

He shook his head and walked with her towards the drawing-room. At the door she paused and held out her hand.

'Good night,' she said and moved across the room to re-join the tall young man who had failed at Graham's audition. He remembered now that the name of the actor was Simon Tasker. With his broad smile and smooth, innocent face he was certainly attractive. Graham searched round the crowd and found Mae Millington near the bar.

'Thanks for a splendid evening,' he said.

'You're not going already?'

14

'I'm afraid I must. I've got some work to do before I leave for Paris.'

Mae chuckled and pressed her knee affectionately against him.

'Work, Graham?' she murmured.

He grinned and kissed her. 'Good night, love,' he said.

He could see Mary Pritchard – another recent mistress – advancing towards him with a glitter in her eyes. He turned away quickly and he left alone, without saying good-bye to anyone else.

2

NEXT morning Graham was awakened by the revving of a car engine outside his flat. He had been dreaming that he was driving through the New Forest with Vicky in an early bull-nosed Morris. She was singing an aria that probably came from *La Traviata* whilst he was steering the car with one hand and eating fish-and-chips with the other. They had decided to stop in a clearing because Vicky had seen some foxgloves that she wanted to pick. But although they had stopped, the sound of the motor outside, which he had connected with the bull-nosed Morris, continued. When the noise outside no longer tallied with his dream he had woken up.

He looked at his watch. It was half-past seven, and too early to telephone her. He got out of bed and felt for his wallet in the suit he had been wearing. The card she had given him was there and he took it back to bed with him. He enjoyed the idiocy of the situation. He examined her swift, definite handwriting and tried to remember the last time he had woken thinking of someone in this way. Presently he dozed off.

Vaguely, he was aware of the sound of his housekeeper, Mrs Lucas, letting herself into the flat. From her punctuality over the years he knew that it was eight o'clock. A few minutes later she rapped loudly on his door.

'Good mornin'!' she called out.

'Good morning, Mrs Lucas,' he replied, equally cheerfully.

'What would you like for your breakfast this morning, Mr Hadley?'

'I'd love two poached eggs and coffee.'

He waited for her footsteps to move away towards the kitchen and then picked up the telephone. He fumbled among the bedclothes for the card he had been holding and dialled Vicky's number. Her voice answered immediately. He was amazed to find himself nervous.

'Hullo, Vicky,' he said. 'This is Graham Hadley.'

There was a pause for an instant and he felt the dreadful uncertainty he had known at eighteen when telephoning a girl for the first time.

'Hullo,' she said. She sounded a little surprised.

He transferred the receiver to his other hand. 'I said I'd call you this morning before I left for Paris. I'm ringing to ask if you'd like to fly out and join me. It's not as wicked a proposal as it sounds. We could always stay at separate hotels. And be quite sure I'd send you a return ticket.'

Her voice was both cautious and firm. 'I'm afraid it's impossible,' she said. 'Even if I was mad keen to come I couldn't, because I've got a job. And just now I'm off to the office.'

'Where do you work?'

'In an advertising firm. I'm a secretary.'

He tried to think quickly.

'I suppose there's no chance of your having an attack of spring fever or something?'

She laughed. 'It's very kind of you, Graham. But I don't live in cuckoo-land. It might be fun to come, but it really is out of the question.'

He leaned out of bed to take a cigarette from the box on a nearby table. He was pleased that she had called him by his Christian name.

'Do you work on Saturday mornings?'

'No, thank heavens.'

'Then if you like I'll send you tickets for a private showing

17

of my latest film. It's in Wardour Street at eleven o'clock this next Saturday as ever is.'

He flicked his lighter but the flint was worn and would not spark.

'That would be marvellous,' she said.

The wick caught and he lit his cigarette and inhaled quickly.

'I'd love you to see the film,' he continued. 'I'll send you two tickets so that you can bring someone. But just one thing. Do drop me a line to let me know what you think of it.'

Vicky at last seemed friendly. 'That's very kind of you,' she said. 'I've never been to a preview before.'

Mrs Lucas came in with the morning papers. He glanced up at her and smiled, then carried on with his conversation.

'If I give you my address in Paris, will you write to me there?'

'Surely.'

'Would you like to take down the name of my hotel?'

Mrs Lucas was staring at him in dismay from across the room. For a moment he thought he must be lying naked above the sheets. He followed her eyes down to his cigarette.

'My housekeeper's reprimanding me for smoking in bed,' he said to Vicky.

Mrs Lucas put down the newspapers on his bed-side table.

'I'm staying at the Hôtel de France et Choiseul. It's in the Rue Saint Honoré quite close to the Ritz. I do look forward to hearing from you. And I hope you'll have dinner with me when I get back from Paris.'

'Fine,' she said briskly. 'But now I must dash for work.'

Mrs Lucas shook her head at him as he put down the receiver.

'You'll burn more holes in those sheets, Mr Hadley,' she announced. 'As sure as eggs is eggs.'

The telephone began to ring, and Mrs Lucas left the bedroom to deal with his breakfast. He waited for a short time before picking up the receiver.

'Graham.' Cole sounded out of breath. 'I've managed to get us seats together on the eleven o'clock plane. I've arranged for a car to pick you up at a quarter to ten. Is that all right?'

Graham wedged the receiver under his chin and took up a newspaper from the bedside table.

'Excellent,' he said. 'That means we'll have time for lunch in Paris before the meeting.' He glanced at the headlines and turned to the back page. He had once admired a stockbroker who could dictate a letter and follow the teleprinter at the same time. Less ambitiously, he now carried on a conversation on the telephone and studied a crossword puzzle.

'Any news?' Cole was asking. 'What gave chez Mae – apart from Mae?'

Graham laughed. He wanted to talk about Vicky, yet at the same time he found himself guarding her name as a secret.

'I played a devastatingly exciting parlour-game of enormous psychological importance,' he said. 'And apart from that, I met a very pretty girl and drank too much.'

He inserted the words Vicky Tollard into two of the blank spaces of the puzzle. To his surprise her name fitted exactly into the pattern.

'What was the girl's name?'

'Vicky Tollard.' He had just written her name, but now it seemed odd. He repeated it to himself several times. He was reluctant to tell Cole anything about her. He dropped the newspaper and took the receiver from under his chin.

'Well, I'd better put on some clothes,' he said. 'I'll see you at the airport. Thanks for calling.'

He got out of bed, crossed into the bathroom and switched on the lights. He went over to the mirror, which was set into the tiled wall above an old-fashioned marble washstand bought in the Portobello Road by the designer of his flat. His face looked hard and bristly. He examined his teeth. They were strong, well-shaped and even, and his dentist complimented himself on their condition three times a year. To cheer himself still further, he turned and displayed himself to the long mirror beside the bath. If he was found one morning with his head cut off and stolen, he thought, they would decide that his body belonged to an extremely virile man of thirty.

He heard Mrs Lucas knock on his bedroom door and put the tray down on his table. While he was under the spray, the telephone rang again. Suddenly he realized that Vicky might be calling to say that she had changed her mind and had found an excuse for not going to her office. He turned off the shower and seized a towel. When the bell stopped ringing he knew that Mrs Lucas had answered on the extension. A moment later there was a knock on the door.

'It's from Paris, Mr Hadley.'

He put on a dressing-gown and picked up the receiver by his bed. The call was from his French agent who wanted three more copies of the outline of the life of Abdel Krim. Luckily he had them in the flat, and he had time to stop the car on his way to London Airport and send flowers to Vicky.

Throughout the day Graham found it difficult to concentrate on even the most trivial chores. By now a picture of Vicky with her forlorn yet arrogant expression had invaded his mind and was smothering his thoughts. Part of him enjoyed this absorption, part of him resented the interference with his work. His secretary had brought down his mail to the airport, and he went through it in the waiting-hall. There were two telegrams, and idiotically, for an instant, he hoped that one of them was from Vicky who might have found out his office address.

'Now what are you up to? Registering the kind of pose that was known as "a brown study" in the novels of my youth?'

As soon as he heard the voice, without moving his head from his papers, he knew that Cole Edwards had arrived. He glanced up and smiled.

'You're looking very spruce this morning,' Graham said.

Cole was wearing a tight-fitting charcoal-grey suit and a black knitted-silk tie with a pale shantung shirt. He was nearing sixty, but his slim figure and alert movements made him seem younger. His thinning grey hair was carefully brushed back from his permanently-tanned face. Graham envied him his obvious zest for pleasure and his enthusiasm for work.

'I may tell you,' Cole said, his eyes blinking behind his square, tortoiseshell spectacles, 'that while you were rapt in concentration our flight number was called. So pop your papers in your bag and let's join the swarming herds at the gate.'

'One thing one can state for sure,' Cole said as they walked across the tarmac. 'If you travel by plane, you travel steerage.'

On the plane Graham tried to dismiss Vicky from his mind, if only for a while, and by the time they landed at Orly he had read his letters and answered a few of them.

After lunch with Cole at the Grenouille, he drove off to the conference, reminding himself how much depended on

21

the meeting and how little, after all, depended on Vicky. Half an hour later, sitting at a large ebony-topped table, surrounded by the three French film magnates and their colleagues and assistants, he felt that he had won back his self-control. As he spoke, he watched their faces and knew that he was impressing them with his simple exposition of the problems involved in making the film of Abdel Krim's life, using Morocco as the main location. After he had talked for an hour they sat down to discuss figures, and soon after six the conference ended. He took a taxi back to his hotel, feeling tired but confident. Cole was waiting for him in the sitting-room between their two bedrooms.

'How did it go?'

'They're definitely interested,' Graham said, helping himself to a drink from the bottle of Sanserres that Cole had ordered. 'They'll ring Hollywood tonight. We'll know the position within the next few days.'

Graham tossed his coat on to the back of a chair, loosened his tie, and settled himself on a Récamier sofa.

'And are their French backers still playing ball?'

'They're willing to put up forty per cent of the money. But they want to be in on the story conference tomorrow, so you'll have to do your stuff in a big way.'

'You can trust your old friend,' Cole said. 'I presume they all speak English?'

'At least they can understand it.'

'Then you don't have to worry. I'll slay them.'

Graham propped up his head on a cushion and tried to make his voice sound casual. 'Incidentally,' he said, 'have any cables arrived for me?'

Cole's eyes moved towards him.

'No,' he replied. 'Are you expecting one?'

Graham shook his head. He began to work out the earliest day that a letter could reach him. He calculated

22

that if Vicky wrote to him on Sunday the letter would reach him by Wednesday. Cole had crossed to the window and was gazing down into the courtyard. He turned abruptly to face Graham.

'*What* was the name of the girl you met at Mae Millington's party?'

Graham sat up. 'Vicky Tollard,' he said, less evenly than he would have liked. 'Why do you ask?'

Cole smiled. 'I just wanted to see your reaction.'

Graham stifled a childish annoyance. 'And what *was* my reaction?'

'I really didn't notice.' His eyes stayed on Graham, and his smile grew broader.

'Well, as it so happens you're right,' Graham said quietly. 'And there's nothing whatever I can do about it.'

Cole walked to the door. 'Any old how, it makes a change,' he said as he turned the handle. 'And I'm a rare one for changes.'

The door closed behind him, and Graham let his head sink back on the cushion. He had always admired Cole's sense of timing.

Like most successful people in the film industry, Graham lived in a world of fluctuating decisions and uncertainty, and in recent years he had built up a resistance against the anxiety of waiting – whether for a cable from Los Angeles or a suit from his tailor. Thus, when the *chasseur* brought up his mail on Wednesday morning, he was pleased to note that he was almost unperturbed. He went slowly through the envelopes and saw that most of them had been forwarded from his office. The only two letters addressed directly to the hotel were electrically typed in green, and he knew that they came from his agent in London. Firmly, he told himself that he was stupid to expect Vicky to write so soon. It was possible that she had lost his address or might not write at all – and firmly he forced himself to abide by his decision that he would not telephone the number she had given him until she had written to him.

On Thursday morning there was still no letter, and he found himself working out childish explanations for the delay while he listened to Cole reading him the rough draft he had made of the final sequence of the film. Supposing she had written to him from her office on Monday and had posted the letter on Tuesday . . . He looked up to find Cole watching him with a hint of amusement showing in the wrinkles at the corner of his eyes.

'As I was saying,' Cole murmured, peering at him over his spectacles, 'Abdel Krim's exiled in Cairo but he wants to get back to his birthplace way up in the Rif mountains before he dies.'

Graham's mind switched back to his work.

'How are you going to *show* that?' he asked. 'Isn't our whole problem that the last years of his life are rather an anti-climax? Oughtn't we to end with the triumph of the cause for which he'd fought like a lion?'

'Right,' Cole said patiently. 'Then let's try it that way. But can we do it over lunch, because yours truly is starving?'

Graham was alone that afternoon when a page-boy came into the sitting-room with a salver in his hand, and he knew instinctively that her letter had arrived. He picked up the envelope and recognized her spiky but firm writing

24

with its upright capitals. He overtipped the boy and ripped open the letter. He read it through slowly twice:

Dear Graham,

My dilemma was whether to sound pompous and call you Mr Hadley or presumptuous and call you Graham. Anyhow, I promised to write to you and this I am doing.

I loved your film, and I only hope that it has the success that it deserves – to coin a phrase. I went on Saturday with Simon Tasker who suspected that perhaps the market-stall of flowers that you sent me might have affected my judgement! Thanks enormously. I really do love them, and the flat – for once – smells divine. I'm most grateful.

There seems very little else for me to say. Except that about our meeting again, the ball's in your court. I like you, and I'd love to dine with you one night. But if we do meet again, you mustn't expect me to fall in love with you and you mustn't expect me to go to bed with you.

Yours,

Vicky.

Graham had refused to allow himself to guess what she might write to him, and he was not disappointed with the letter, for it gave him some hope. At least he would be able to meet her again. And he was determined to establish some form of relationship. He was old enough to know that you can sift through the sand for ever looking for a particular shell and find dozens of pretty ones but not the one you want.

He rang down to the reception for a cable-form. The boy who brought it waited while he wrote it out in block letters and read it through to make sure it was in order:

ALL TERMS AGREED WILL MEET YOU BAR HERMITAGE CLUB CURZON STREET 8.30 TUESDAY LOVE GRAHAM.

3

THEY had arrived early on Tuesday morning at Orly airport, and Cole had disappeared in the direction of the bar. Graham wandered round the glass-fronted little shops clustered together in the centre of the vast hall. His eyes roamed along lines of duty-free scents and lingerie, but he saw nothing that he could be sure would please her until he noticed a Christian Dior silk square. He looked round to make sure that Cole was not watching him, went in and bought it, and concealed it in his brief-case so as to avoid Cole's smile.

In Upper Grosvenor Street that evening he took a taxi that happened to be passing, though he had time to walk the short distance to the Hermitage Club. His secretary had wrapped up the box that contained the scarf and he carried it in his hand. He had decided not to take out the Bentley because he could not afford – that evening – to be distracted by the problem of finding a place to park it at each place they visited.

'Good evening, Mr Hadley,' the commissionaire said as he opened the door. 'It's a lovely evening.'

'It certainly is,' Graham replied. He had been looking forward to it for over a week.

The bar was not crowded and he took a stool at the far end and put the box down beside him. From concealed speakers in the ceiling above him, a record of a Bach cantata played as jazz was softly filtered into the room. The young Italian barman put down the plate of sliced pizza he had been handing round and came over to take his order.

26

'Large whisky as usual, Mr Hadley?'

'Thanks, Angelo.'

He could see from the reflection of the buhl clock in the looking-glass behind the bar that it was ten minutes to nine. He glanced down at the stool beside him to make sure the present was still there. His drink arrived, and he sipped it slowly, wondering at the foolishness of his excitement and yet enjoying it.

A few minutes before nine o'clock Vicky appeared in the doorway. Graham slid off the stool and went to meet her. She was wearing the same plain black dress she had worn at the party. Her face looked narrower than it had been in his memory and yet she seemed more beautiful. She smiled at him as he came to greet her.

'I'm always terrified of going into bars alone,' she said.

He took her arm. 'I'm sorry. If I'd known I'd have driven round to your flat.'

They sat down at a table between the bar and the restaurant. Angelo hovered benignly over them.

What will you drink?' Graham asked her.

He was so fascinated by her presence and by the prospect of a whole evening alone with her that every word uttered now took on a ludicrous importance.

'Vodka and tonic, please.'

'I bought you a little present in Paris,' he announced after Angelo had left.

Two furrows of surprise appeared between her eyebrows. He reached for the packet but it had gone. He looked down and saw that it had slipped on to the floor. He laughed as he stretched down for it and handed it to her with a slight bow of the head. She unwrapped the paper and saw a grey cardboard box on which the words 'Christian Dior' were embossed in gold. He was happy to watch her face as she took out the scarf.

27

'It's beautiful,' she said. 'But you really shouldn't. . . . It's too kind of you.'

'It's my first present to you,' he said. 'And if it has to be the last, I'm sure I'll remember it far longer than you will.'

Angelo appeared with her drink and a plate of pizza and left them quickly because the bar was filling up.

'Where would you like to dine?' Graham asked. 'If I say that London is at your feet it will sound corny. But the idea's there just the same.'

His eyes were on her lips as she smiled.

'Would you like to eat here?' he continued. 'The food's as good as anywhere.'

Her eyes wandered towards the restaurant with its Venetian sconces on the dark red walls and the twin chandeliers above the lamp-lit tables. She hesitated.

'To be honest,' she said, 'this place . . . well, it's smart. But somehow – I don't want to sound rude – somehow it's not quite *me*.'

'The choice is yours.'

'You don't mind if I choose?'

'I want you to,' he said. But he was disappointed that she had not liked his favourite restaurant.

'I've got a friend who's just opened a restaurant in Chelsea,' she said. 'I haven't been there yet, but I'm told the place is quite fun, so perhaps we could kill two birds with one stone?'

'Certainly,' he said. 'But let's have one more drink here first.'

Graham had been surprised by her indifference to the Hermitage, for it was fashionable and used by celebrities who could eat there without having the eyes of a whole

28

room fixed on them, and he had hoped she would be impressed by it. The restaurant to which she now took him was exactly what he had expected. It was called La Carabine and was situated half-way down the King's Road. He opened the door for her and pushed aside a heavy leather curtain and they entered a room which looked as if it had been decorated for a gala night at a munitions factory. Pistols and rifles were hung against black drapery on the walls, and on each table stood a thick crimson wax candle throwing a lurid light on to black-and-white check table-cloths. They were shown to a table in a corner and sat down on uncomfortable wooden chairs.

'Is your friend here?' Graham asked Vicky.

'I think he's in the kitchen. He told me he was having a little trouble with his chef.'

'Then let's hope one of them can cook,' Graham said.

A waiter in a white tunic with a silver-handled dagger tucked into the sash round his waist brought them the menu. It was in the shape of an eighteenth-century pistol and printed in Gothic type and almost impossible to read in the flickering light. Graham held the candle towards her. Vicky studied the card and then smiled at the waiter.

'I'll have Soupe Marseillaise and Steak au Poivre,' she said.

'I'll have the same,' Graham added, not wishing to strain his eyes. He had begun to dislike the place. The décor was overpowering and its effect claustrophobic. The waiter handed him the wine list which was fortunately printed in clear type.

'Red or white?' he asked her.

'I don't drink much wine. You choose.'

He ordered a bottle of Chambertin. For a while Vicky was silent. From the dimly-lit table next to them came fragments of conversation.

'The trouble is that people try to be amusing and one can't retaliate.'

'One simply shouldn't make the effort. After all, one has so many other things to do . . .'

'I find that knowledge only attracts me if it's utterly and completely useless.' The voice was reedy and the accent carefully primed. 'For instance, did you know that in Africa there exists a parasitic tick that lives on the upper eyelid of a rhinoceros and feeds upon its tears?'

'Talking of parasitic ticks,' a deep blurred voice said, 'who's going to order the next bottle of wine?'

'Well, it's certainly not *my* turn.'

Vicky spoke. 'Isn't this place fun? My friend designed it himself.'

Graham smiled. Perhaps he was getting old. He offered her a cigarette from his gold case. It had been a present from the company for which he had directed his first film, and they could well afford it, he recalled, because the film had made a sixty per cent profit – unlike *The Strawberry Patch* which had not yet paid back its cost. The trouble with shooting a high-budget film on location was that bad weather could add a hundred thousand pounds to the expense in a matter of weeks.

'Tell me something about your life,' Vicky said. She might have been reading his thoughts.

As Graham lit her cigarette and then his own, he decided to be light, almost flippant.

'There's not much to tell,' he replied. 'I came from a large family. I've got three brothers and two sisters. My father was a chemist who was too mean to buy contraceptives and never discovered how to make them. We led a pretty dull life at home, which was in the suburbs of Birmingham. All I wanted to do was to leave school and find a job so that I could make my own way in life and get away from the Midlands. At sixteen I was given a job in some local film laboratories . . .'

She listened with both hands supporting her chin. The candle-light made her eyes dark and accentuated the oval shape of her face.

'You must be wonderfully photogenic,' he said. 'Have you ever thought of going into films?'

'When I did a modelling course last year, the agent wanted to arrange a screen test. But I'd be desperately self-conscious. It's not my line of country.'

'That's a pity,' he said, 'because I'd have enjoyed helping you.'

He saw that her lack of interest was genuine, and he found himself comparing her with the girls he usually took out. Most of them would have been in his bed with a vision of their names billed above the film title long before he had made any definite offer.

'And after the laboratories?' she asked.

'When I was nineteen I got married to the girl next door. I'm still married – I've got two kids. Then the war came and I was called up and spent three relatively uneventful years in the Signals in the Middle East. After I was demobbed I was restless, and I managed to get myself attached to a documentary film unit that was going out to West Africa. The assistant director had an attack of malaria on location outside Dakar. So I got his job.'

'What went wrong with your marriage?'

Graham fingered his wine-glass.

'I hope you don't mind my asking,' she said.

'Not at all,' he replied, and as he spoke he was surprised to find that it was true. He no longer minded speaking of his marriage, for he no longer cared. 'What went wrong? Well – to be honest with myself – I suppose I did. You see, I made good. I changed, and she wouldn't. But don't think

I had my success because of talent. I promise you it was mainly luck. I was offered a job directing a second feature. I did my best with a ghastly story and a script that was worse, and when I'd finished the studio shelved the whole film. But then came my lucky break. Another picture they'd made turned out to be a complete flop, so they decided to release mine. I'd had a new approach as well as a good cameraman. The film was a success with the critics and did well at the box-office. I was launched. Within three years I was making more money a month than I'd previously earned in a year.'

Graham poured more wine into their glasses.

'I was working most of the time in London, of course. But Joyce wouldn't leave home. She was still a simple girl, but I was no longer a simple boy. There were scenes and tears, and between hysterical recriminations and alcoholic reunions we drifted apart. I wasn't the person she had married, and Joyce wasn't the person I wanted as a wife. So she still lives in our neat little house in Birmingham – with the peroxide and the curlers and the endless cups of tea with the neighbours.'

He stubbed out his cigarette in the ashtray which was also shaped like a pistol. Suddenly he felt guilt for having been disloyal to the girl whose young body he had held so passionately over twenty years ago.

'You must realize that she's got a far better nature than I have,' he concluded tritely in atonement.

The soup came and Graham could distinctly smell glue. As he swallowed a spoonful of the thick red broth with two pieces of cod floating in it he remembered that glue could be made out of fishbones. He put down his spoon.

'What are you staring at?' she asked.

Graham smiled. 'Your eyes. Have you got your contact lenses in?'

32

'Yes.'

'One could never tell. They don't seem to affect the expression of your eyes at all.'

'They don't. That's half the point of them.'

Graham began to eat a roll of bread.

'Tell me about yourself,' he said.

'What kind of things?'

'For instance, how old are you?'

'Eighteen.'

He felt a stab of sadness. He was dining with a child.

'Why are you frowning?' Vicky asked.

'Because you're so very young,' he said. 'Have you any brothers or sisters?'

'I had one brother but he died at six.'

She took a spoonful of soup.

'You know, I've really very little to tell,' she said. 'My parents live in Wiltshire. I went to school at a rather grand local convent.'

'Are you still a Catholic?'

'My parents are . . . Well, I stayed at the convent until I was thirteen – when I was expelled for using a four-letter word on the hockey field.'

Graham laughed. 'Wasn't that a little severe?'

'Not really. You see, we were playing another school, and some parents complained to the Reverend Mother. So then my father sent me to another convent in Switzerland where I could use all the bad language I liked because almost nobody else spoke English. I stayed there for three years and then came back to England and took a secretarial course in Bath. I was down there about a year and then I did the modelling course I told you about.'

'You prefer secretarial work to modelling?'

'No,' Vicky said, 'but it's more secure.'

33

'Are your parents still in Wiltshire?'

'Yes. My father's quite a big solicitor in Shaftesbury.'

Suddenly her face was sad, and her eyes seemed veiled.

'Don't your parents object to you careering round London all by yourself?'

Vicky smiled. Her teeth were very small and white.

'They're not awfully keen on it,' she said. 'But I share a flat with a girl friend who's madly respectable and is training to be a hospital nurse. And that cheers them up a bit. . . . You know, I think you'd like my Ma. She's got a great sense of humour and a wonderful way with horses.'

Vicky was silent. Her eyes were veiled once again. Suddenly she laughed.

'In Cannes once, I took my Ma on to the nudist beach,' she said. 'And she got stung by a wasp on the behind. She's got a huge bottom has my Mamma. She tries to cut down on starch, but she's got a passion for apple pies. When I first came to London she was a bit worried. But when she heard I was sharing the flat with another girl, she felt better.'

While Vicky told him about her respectable friend whose name was Muriel and who sounded precisely the kind of staid, dull girl he would welcome as a room-mate for Vicky, the steak arrived. It was excellent but cold, and he ate half of it. He noticed that Vicky was only making a pretence of eating.

'Would you like me to order something else?'

'No thanks. This is fine.' He saw that she did not intend to let him see her disappointment.

Later, when Muriel's virtuous character and background had been established beyond doubt and he had asked for the bill, some tepid coffee arrived. The first part of the evening had not been a success. He must now lead her gently towards the second stage.

34

'I thought we might go on to some night-club,' he suggested.

'That would be fine.'

Graham smiled into her solemn eyes.

'You don't sound very enthusiastic.'

'It's not that. It's just that when people spend money on taking me out to a night-club, I always feel a bit guilty if I don't enjoy myself. What's more, I believe there are lots of others who react the same way. Sometimes I feel that a night-club merely consists of fifty people who are all thinking, "This is really *living* and I should be having a marvellous time".'

'You're too intelligent to feel guilty. There's no reason why you *should* be happy in any particular place,' he said, feeling rather sententious. 'You may be happier in a Wimpy bar than in the Four Seasons. But in my view, if you're with someone you like, it's only a means towards an end – which is to have a good time.'

The night was warm. The pavement still exuded the heat of an unusually fine May day, and the stars were shining. They walked slowly along the King's Road until they found a taxi. Graham gave the driver the name of a small night-club in Berkeley Square where he hoped there was little chance of meeting anyone he knew. He wanted to be alone with her. He had chosen the club himself in case Vicky announced that she had another friend who had just opened a night-spot.

They settled down at their table. Graham was glad he had chosen a place where they could talk without having to shout above a band. The coloured pianist was playing jazz with delicacy and tenderness as if he had composed each tune himself. His rhythm was instinctive and his technique superb. Graham remembered hearing that he had once given a recital of classical music at the Wigmore Hall. His lean face was motionless, and his large eyes stared ahead into space, oblivious of the crowded room. Graham determined to try to engage him for the next night-club sequence he had to direct.

'Shall we drink some champagne?' he asked.

'Would you mind if I went back to vodka?'

'Not at all. I'll join you.'

While they waited for their drinks to arrive, Graham asked her to dance. As they moved on to the floor, he realized that this was the first time he had held her and almost the first time he had touched her. She danced without effort, letting herself relax against him. He felt an intense warmth and excitement from her. It was a sensation that he thought had become dulled over the years, and he knew more clearly than before that his instinct when he first saw her at the party had been right.

The pianist stopped playing, letting the music fade away into soft chords, nodded to himself vaguely, and wandered towards the bar. Vicky and Graham went back to the table on which a bottle of vodka was standing, and the waiter filled their glasses. Graham watched her eyes move round the room.

'Feeling guilty?'

Vicky smiled. 'Heavens no. It's just the kind of club I like.'

He could still feel the physical awareness with which she had filled him while they were dancing, as if some chemical had reacted in him, and for a moment he was afraid of the anguish to which it might lead. He switched his mind back to their conversation earlier in the dismal restaurant.

'Weren't your parents a bit cross when you got expelled from the convent?' he asked.

'Ma pretended to be, but secretly I think she found it rather a joke. I don't know what my father thought about it. . . . But then I don't really understand him. When I was a little girl my Pa was a terrific disciplinarian. For instance, no one was allowed to read the morning papers until he'd seen them, and I used to have to ask if I could leave the table. He's mellowed with the years, of course. I think as he grew older he became aware it was his own life that was passing as well as mine. Anyway, he stopped worrying about the papers and meals became quite informal.'

She drank and put down her glass.

'I feel that sometimes he regrets he ever married,' she said. 'I don't think my parents were ever in love. It just seemed a good idea at the time.'

Graham refilled her glass and ordered more tonic water. He noticed that she was drinking as much as he was.

'It's funny,' she said, 'I can drink gallons of vodka, and it doesn't have the slightest effect on me. . . . Don't smile. It's true.'

'Are you fond of your father?'

'I think I first began to love him when his attitude changed. I expected him to be livid about my expulsion. I know it wasn't very important but a lot of parents would have gone up the wall. He's too human to inspire filial respect. But that makes him all the easier to love. He's quite attractive in his way. And we have to be awfully careful with the maids we have because they all get crushes on him.'

'How old is he?'

'Nearly fifty, I think.'

'What does he look like?'

She eyed him thoughtfully.

'Medium height, strands of grey in his hair, rather dark complexion, broad forehead, brown eyes, and fairly heavy shoulders, though he's not really tall.'

'I an way,' Graham said, 'he sounds a bit like me – to look at, that is.'

Her eyes stayed on him. She picked up her glass and drank.

'Yes, I s'pose he is in a way.' She frowned, as if the thought had displeased her, and was silent for a while.

'Do you know, I had a marvellous nurse called Emmy,' she began abruptly. 'We had little white stones running along a border in the garden, and every morning before breakfast I used to walk round examining each stone. And if I'd been good the previous day, the fairies would have left a couple of sweets on one of them. It was wonderfully exciting. But one morning when I got out of bed I spotted Emmy crossing the lawn carrying a box of chocolates. And I knew that Emmy didn't eat chocolates. Well, I didn't let on for weeks that I'd found out her trick. But then I did something wrong and she got very cross with me. So I drew the ace from my sleeve, and I told her that I didn't believe in fairies *at all*, and I told her I knew she'd put the goodies out. Mind you, I made a great mistake because there were never any sweets on the stones again.'

'There's a moral somewhere in that story,' Graham said. 'But I can't for the life of me think what it is.'

'Emmy's our housekeeper now and we often joke about it. She's an old pet. She's got straggling white hair and moles on her cheek. And I just adore her.'

Vicky raised her glass to her lips, then looked at him in astonishment. Suddenly she began to giggle.

'I have to tell you,' she said, 'that one of my contact lenses has just fallen into my glass.'

38

He was surprised that she was so unconcerned.

'You're joking,' he said.

She put down her drink, put her little finger in the glass, and picked out something. It was a small, almost invisible piece of plastic. She then popped it in her mouth and smiled at his amazement.

'It's when one of them falls into minestrone soup that you have to worry,' she said, removing the tiny convex object from her tongue and balancing it on her index finger. Then she bowed her head slightly, raised her hand and quickly inserted the lens in place.

'Do they fall out frequently?' he asked.

'Good Lord, no. Once every blue moon. Usually when I'm tired.'

'And are you tired now?'

She smiled at him.

'Not one bit,' she said.

He was watching her, now, across the table, examining her unlined forehead and small nose, observing carefully the long upper lip above the wide mouth, noting the way her hair fell around the delicate skin of her neck which was slightly too long, registering each detail of her face as if this profound concentration could slow down the passage of time that was moving so rapidly. Meanwhile, he asked her questions, searching for common interests they could share, but apart from the stage and the screen there seemed to be few. Yet their conversation flowed easily and without any check, as if it were stimulated by the sympathy which he was convinced had now been established between Vicky and himself. For a while her veneer of sophistication could make him forget the disparity in their ages until she made some impetuous or naïve remark that reminded him with a jolt of her youth. He noticed that she was drinking steadily, without showing any sign of getting drunk, and he hoped that any lingering traces of the hostility she had displayed when they first met would be washed away with each swallow.

Vicky looked at her watch.

'What time would you say it was?' she asked.

'One o'clock?'

'I'd have said so too. But it's nearly three.'

'Should we go?'

She sighed. 'I suppose we should.'

He called for the bill. He had drunk sufficiently to see the situation with a detached clarity. He wanted her more than he had ever wanted anyone before. But he knew that he must keep control over his desire, for tenderness and the wish to protect her were so mingled with his passion that he was determined not to risk losing her.

'Would you like to come back for a night-cap?' he asked as they stood outside on the pavement waiting for the commissionaire to bring a taxi. He deliberately avoided using the word 'flat' in case the word had some wicked connotation in Wiltshire.

She was wearing her ocelot-skin coat loosely over her shoulders and leaning on his arm.

'I'll come back for a drink,' she said.

He was careful not to touch her as he took her coat and laid it on the side-table. He followed her into the flat and watched her gaze as it wandered over the discreetly-lit living-room.

'But it's wonderful,' she said. 'I adore the spaciousness

of it all. I love the different levels and the mixture of styles.'

He did not reply, but for the first time he decided that the money he had paid his decorator had been worth while. He moved to the drink-table.

'Do you like jazz?' he asked.

'I'm mad on Bechet.'

He brought her a vodka and crossed over to the record-player.

'Good. I'll put one on.'

Suddenly, as the quiet music broke the silence of the two hi-fi speakers, Graham felt he might be arranging the sound-track of a French film. He took his drink and sat down beside her.

'How long have you been in London?' he asked.

'Nearly a year.'

'And you've been around?'

Her solemn eyes were fixed on him.

'Yes,' she said. 'I've been around.'

'Meaning all that the phrase implies?'

'Pretty well.'

He stared down at his glass.

'Does that shock you?' she asked.

'No.'

'They're funny,' she said.

'Who are?'

'Men.'

'Why so?'

'Well, all of you believe it's perfectly all right for *you* to have a fling when you're eighteen. But when a girl does, you think it's all wrong.'

'Perhaps because we're selfish.'

'Or don't understand about girls.'

Graham was silent. His mouth felt dry and he took up

41

his glass and drank. He tried to listen to the music as if its gentle rhythm could regulate the uneven beats of his heart. The conversation was slipping away from his grasp, gliding towards dangerous terrain. He made an effort to regain control over the scene.

'What kind of office do you work in?' he could hear his voice asking.

'Advertising. I told you. I'm secretary to the boss.'

'What's his name?'

'Pleydell. George Pleydell. Do you know him?'

'I don't think so.'

'Tall, slim, grey eyes, wonderfully soft voice, and a nice smile. He's quite a charmer. And he's super to work for, because he never gets cross.'

'Has he made advances to you?'

Vicky laughed. 'Of course he has.'

'And?'

'And I made it clear that it was no go.'

'Why – if he's so charming?'

'Why? Because he's old. He's well over forty.'

'Thank you,' Graham said, smiling.

'I'm sorry. That was stupid of me. But you do know what I mean?'

'Not quite.'

'Well, I only go around with boys of my own age.'

'And you sleep with them?'

Vicky looked up at him, her eyes wide in surprise.

'If we're fond of each other and if they're attractive to me, then of course I do.'

'Why "of course"?'

'Well, if two young people are made for each other and they can find a place to kip, they go to bed together. Didn't they in your day?'

Graham decided to be flippant once more.

'It's too long ago to remember,' he said.

Vicky sipped her drink.

'Did you know that whenever you're slightly annoyed, you play with your ring?' she asked. 'I noticed it in the restaurant when the soup was so bad. And did you know that you have terribly sensitive hands? I always look at people's hands. They tell you so much more than their face does.'

'How many boys have you been to bed with?'

Vicky gazed at him solemnly.

'Three,' she said after a pause. 'Three, so far.'

'And was one of them Simon Tasker?'

'Do you think I'd tell you if he was?'

'Have you never been with a man?'

'No.'

'You've never tried?'

'No. Why should I?'

'Because you might enjoy it.'

He could hear his voice speaking, but it seemed to come from far away. Vicky was staring at the Guillaumin on the wall opposite.

'Graham,' she said, 'I must tell you that I meant what I said in my letter about not going to bed with you. You're very attractive, and I'm sure you're never short of a bed-mate. It's nothing to do with you personally. It's a question of preference. And I've told you. If I do sleep with someone, it's with a boy of my own age and because I want to.'

She turned her head away from the picture and looked at him.

'Are you angry with me?'

'No.'

'You see, I do like you. I like you very much. But I just feel it wouldn't work. In fact, I'm sure it wouldn't. But if

43

you ask me, I'd love to come out with you again. I'll come out with you any night you say.'

Graham got up from the sofa.

'Where are you going?' she asked in a quiet, lazy voice.

'I forgot to put any ice in our drinks.'

On his way out of the room he picked up a Regency silver-gilt box with Adam and Eve engraved on its lid and placed it on the table in the hall. This was his signal to Mrs Lucas who arrived every morning at eight that he was sleeping late and did not want to be disturbed. At the sight of the box in the hall Mrs Lucas would make her way to a little sitting-room at the far end of the flat and remain there until the bell rang. It was an arrangement that had worked for over seven years.

When he returned with the ice-bucket, Vicky was sitting in exactly the same position. Her eyes turned towards him. They were strangely without expression. He put a cube of ice in her glass. He rested his hand against the back of the sofa for a moment, bent forward and kissed her on the forehead.

'Be sure that the last thing I'll do,' he said, 'is to try to make you do something you don't want to.'

He sat down beside her. He put his arm on her shoulder and gently turned her head towards him. And as he watched her face he knew that he could remove the drink from her hand and put it on the table by the lamp.

A few moments later, she did not resist when he took her hand and led her across the room.

4

IT seemed to him that long before he awoke he was conscious that she was lying beside him, though she had moved away from him and their bodies were no longer touching. He leaned forward and looked down at her. In sleep she had an innocence that made her seem untouchable, and he placed a pillow behind his head and lay there watching her.

Presently she stirred. She looked up at him with the sad expression in her eyes of a child who has been punished unexpectedly by its parents.

'I was awfully drunk last night,' she said quietly. 'You do know that, don't you?'

He smiled at her. 'I do know that,' he said. 'But you're not drunk now.'

He took her in his arms and kissed her, but she did not respond. His hands began to stroke the soft skin of her narrow shoulders and to slide down her slender body, and as want began to move in him he remembered with a stab of pain that his relationship with her was impermanent and strewn with hazards. It was even possible that he would never see her again. Then he held her pressed close to him and embraced her in the same desperate way that he had made love to his wife, some twenty-five years ago, on the last night of his embarkation leave. He longed to explain to Vicky the wonder he felt at this experience of re-birth, but he knew that it was impossible for him to put into words. Her arms had begun to move now, and fingers were stroking his hair.

.   .   .   .   .   .

When she came out of the bathroom, Vicky was fully dressed. Graham had made coffee and was sitting in the living-room in a dressing-gown.

'Can I pour you a cup?'

Her face was stiff as she looked at him.

'I don't think I have time,' she said. 'I have to go back to my flat to change, and it'll make me late for the office.'

He supposed that she had made her voice sound off-hand in order to conceal nervousness or perhaps embarrassment. He stood up and moved towards her.

'I must go,' she said. 'Would you mind getting my coat?'

He walked slowly into the hall. He wanted time to think.

'Can we meet for dinner tonight?' he asked when he came back into the room.

Vicky was silent.

'Shall we say the Caprice at nine?' He was puzzled by her mood.

At last she spoke. 'All right,' she said in a flat voice.

After she had left him the worries that had been lurking at the back of his mind surged forward. He knew he had behaved badly on almost every level. Even a few minutes ago he could have slipped on some clothes and walked down into the street with her to find a taxi. But he had expected her to stay for a while, drinking coffee with him. He had forgotten that she was not dressed for her office. And above all his worries came the fear that he might have made her feel cheap.

He sat facing the doorway with his back to the partition that gave on to the restaurant. He allowed himself a drink every quarter of an hour that he waited for her. From time to time a friend would come through the entrance and move across the room to greet him. Graham would smile and refuse a drink, and he would be congratulated on *The Strawberry Patch* and asked his immediate plans. All the time he kept an eye on the door.

He had been afraid she would not come, and after his fourth drink – when she was three-quarters of an hour late – he asked Mario not to keep his table and decided he would wait for her until ten o'clock and then leave. His eyes had seldom left the doorway, but with his last drink he turned and watched the faces of the people eating. He could feel himself sinking into a gloom that was increased by the whisky he had drunk on an empty stomach. His thoughts drifted back to the time shortly after the break-up of his marriage when he had decided firmly that he would never allow himself to care again. Since then he had become used to casual affairs, though inevitably he had begun to find less excitement in each new body, but his need to love and to be loved had obstinately persisted. He now confessed to himself that in Vicky he had found the person for whom he had been searching more desperately than he had been willing to admit.

He finished his drink and glanced towards the bar. Then he sprang up from his table, for the young girl standing there with her back turned to the room was Vicky, and she was wearing the familiar black dress. As he hurried towards her the girl turned, and he saw that it was a stranger. He stared at her in dismay, loathing the slim young girl as if she had betrayed him. He signed his bill and left quickly.

An hour after he reached his flat, he rang her number for the third time, but there was still no reply. His living-room seemed large and empty, and he wondered how he had ever been able to live in the place for seven years without a permanent companion. As he poured himself a drink he decided that apart from his slight fame in the unreal microcosm of the film-world he was a middle-aged failure, unable to sustain an emotional relationship for any length of time, unable to command any lasting devotion. A gloomy, grim self-portrait slid into his mind. It was of an ageing man with a brittle facile charm, surrounded at parties by casual friends and hangers-on, possessing a long list of telephone numbers of girls who would go to bed with him in the hope of a part in his next film; a man who could exude the aroma of success without apparent effort; a popular contented-looking man who now sat alone in a big high-ceilinged impersonal room with a glass of whisky in his hand. His life, he saw, had followed the pattern of his work as a director – three or four months of passionate enthusiasm and sleepless nights followed by a flat period of calm until another project came along which in its turn would absorb his energies completely and then be forgotten.

He put down his glass and walked into his bedroom. He now hated himself for having been so ruthless in his ambition. In her simple and unsophisticated way his wife had been wise to fear the change of background. Certainly he had too easily adopted the morality of a manner of living that allowed him to treat lovers in the same way as his work, leaving them as soon as he was satisfied.

5

H E was ready when the studio car called for him at eight o'clock, and as the old Humber wove its way like a turtle between the shoals of traffic he let his mind enumerate once more the reason why she had not met him the previous evening. Perhaps he had made her feel cheap by seducing her into his bed on the first night that he had taken her out, or he had let her drink too much and she blamed him, or he should have offered to drive her home in the morning – after all, she had said that she would be late for work – or perhaps she was ill.

When he arrived at the studio, he asked his secretary to track down a Mr George Pleydell's office telephone number. He then rang it himself on his private line.

'Could I speak to Miss Tollard?' he asked.

'Miss Tollard?' the switchboard-girl repeated in a bored professional voice that he was sure she did not use at home. 'Miss Tollard? I'll see if she's available.'

He began to look through the papers on his desk and noticed with a dull throb of disappointment that the box-office receipts of *The Strawberry Patch* were falling. You could have reviews and packed houses in Leicester Square, but until you got out into the provinces, no one could really tell.

'I'm afraid Miss Tollard's not available,' the harsh efficient voice said in his ear.

Because he was in his own office at his own desk with his own loyal Betty, aged fifty and as placid as a poached egg, in the ante-room next door, because he was the master of all he surveyed unless he glanced out of the west window towards Elstree Studios, Graham was able to sound calm. He even managed to infuse a tender note of gaiety into his voice.

'We're none of us available,' he said. 'But if we had a wildly tempting offer from an up-and-coming pop singer whose records are spread out like pancakes on every household table, we might change our mind.'

'You slay me,' the voice said without altering pitch. 'And what's your name?'

'Sidney Virtuoso.'

'Sidney *what*?'

'Virtuoso. As I never stop telling the Press, that's the name my stepfather gave me when he kicked me out of our house in West Hartlepool – twenty-three years ago. Don't tell me you've never heard of me?'

'Never.' But he detected doubt in the voice.

'Do you never listen in to the Royal Command Performance?'

'Not if I can help it,' the voice said.

'Be that as it may,' Graham said, 'how can I contact Miss Tollard?'

'You can't,' the female voice said contentedly. 'Mr Pleydell's got a conference with the Norwich Union, and they won't be back till five.'

'Well, at least promise me to buy one of my records.'

'I'll think about it,' the voice said, with a final nasal twinge that he hoped might be adenoids. 'Good morning, Mr Virtuoso.'

'That,' he said, 'was the title of my last record,' and he put down the receiver.

In spare moments during the afternoon he dialled the number of her flat several times, knowing that there would be no reply but gaining some satisfaction from knowing that the bell would be ringing in a room she inhabited. At six Cole Edwards put his head round the door. He was wearing tightly-fitting check trousers, a yellow turtle-necked sweater and a dark blue sports jacket. Graham often wondered why he turned up to work at the studio dressed for a day at the races, whereas he appeared at parties in London in clothes suitable for a funeral.

'It's me,' Cole said. 'Are you still busy or can you spare me a moment?'

'I'm through for the day,' Graham said. 'Can you drive back with me?'

'Nothing I'd like more.'

Cole popped his head back into the ante-room.

'Betty, love, cancel my car, will you?' he said. 'I'm driving back to town with me old pal.'

'How's the treatment?' Graham asked.

'Fine. I'll be able to let you have the completed first draft within a week. But then . . . what then?'

'We go through it together, and you start on the script.'

'That's the problem,' Cole said. 'I wonder if I can.'

Graham smiled. He spoke very quietly.

'That's what it says in the contract.'

Cole clapped his hands together.

'Graham,' he said, 'that was perfect. I just adore it when I see that steely look creep into the eyes of our rising young film tycoon.'

'Middle-aged and still struggling.'

'And still an ace charmer – in spite of a faintly peeky look which I detect today,' Cole said. 'No, Graham, don't worry. I'm not taking off for California on my broomstick. I'll stay with dear Abdel Krim until the final fade-out. But I don't feel I can do the script without visiting the location.'

Graham took up the green telephone that communicated with his secretary next door.

'Betty,' he said, 'could you please bring in a carbon of the letter we sent the travel agency?'

'Now what have you got hidden up that sleeve of yours?' Cole asked as Betty walked in briskly with the letter. She was a large shapeless woman who looked as if she had been inflated with a bicycle pump. Her memory was prodigious – she could tell him the names of every actor in each film the studio had made – and her efficiency was astonishing; but her character, Graham felt, had not matured since she was a girl of fifteen. She was coy, gushing, over-enthusiastic, and easily offended. She hero-worshipped producers and film directors but disdained actors.

'Actors are so common,' she would explain. 'Half of them can't even spell. And the airs they give themselves! You'd think they were royalty or something.'

Betty put down the letter on Graham's desk and took up the ashtray and emptied it neatly into the metal waste-paper basket.

'Thank you, Betty,' Graham said and handed the carbon to Cole.

'Your car's at the front when you're ready, Mr Hadley,' Betty said.

Five years ago, he had suggested that she should call him Graham and she had winced and then blushed as if he had made a lewd proposal.

'Oh, no, I couldn't,' she had simpered. 'I really couldn't.'

'Why ever not?'

'Because it wouldn't be correct.'

'But we all call you Betty. Why shouldn't you call some of us by our Christian names?'

'I was with Mr Bardlock for ten years. And he began to

52

call me Betty after the third month. But I'd no more have
called him Hubert than I'd have danced a jig.'

Hubert Bardlock had been the managing director of the
studio and the loudest champion for purity in British films
until he had died of a stroke in a brothel in Pimlico.

'Anything else, Mr Hadley?' Betty asked.

'No, thanks.'

Betty gave Cole a flirtatious leer and tripped out of the
room. Cole handed back the carbon to Graham.

'One jump ahead of me as usual,' he said. 'And a
furnished apartment in Tangier thrown in.'

'I was keeping our Moroccan expedition as a little surprise for you.'

'Will there be just the two of us?'

For an instant Graham was silent. In his mind he could
see Vicky staring at him across the table in the night-club
with a strange expression of longing in her eyes.

'Just the two of us,' he said, rising from his desk. 'Shall
we go down to the car?'

'You're miles away.'

Graham turned round. He had been gazing out of the
car window and he had forgotten that Cole was sitting next
to him.

'I'm sorry,' he said. 'I was just thinking.'

'And to judge from your face they weren't very happy
thoughts.'

'Perhaps not.'

Cole wound up the glass partition between them and the
driver.

'What's wrong?' he asked. 'Tell your old friend.'

The car had pulled up at a set of traffic lights. Graham

53

watched the colours change from red to amber. They seemed to stay on amber for a long time.

'The stupid thing is that I can't even joke about it,' he said.

'Then shall I make a little guess at what it is?' Cole asked.

'If you like.'

'A girl. Am I right?'

'Could be.'

'What was the name of the girl you met at Mae's party? Wasn't it Vicky Tollard?'

'You've got a good memory.'

'And you've fallen for her?'

'Yes,' Graham said. 'In fact, you could say that I was pretty hopelessly in love.'

'Is she an actress?'

'No. She works in an advertising agency.'

'How old is she?'

'Eighteen.'

Cole looked out of the window and Graham saw the reflection of his face in the glass. The age had sounded unfortunately young as he gave it.

'You've met her again recently?' Cole asked.

'Yes.'

'And what subsequently transpired – as they'll say in the police court?'

'I took her out to dine and then we went on to a night-club.'

'And then?'

'We went back to the flat. And that's about all.'

Cole glanced at him and smiled.

'So far, I must confess, it doesn't sound all that tragic,' he said.

'But that was two evenings ago.'

54

'Ah, now we have it.'

'Last night she was supposed to dine with me, but she didn't show up. I waited over an hour. I rang her flat but there was no answer. I thought perhaps she was ill or something. But when I phoned her office today, they said she'd gone with her boss to a conference.'

'Does she know that you're working down at the studio?'

'Yes.'

'And there was no phone call to explain why she didn't turn up?'

'None.'

'It may sound hard,' Cole said, 'and it's bound to prick your ego – I know it always does mine. But I suppose there *is* the possibility that she's just not interested?'

Graham watched the face of a woman who was staring at him from a passing car. He would have cast her in a film as a riding mistress.

'You may be right,' he said. 'But it's awfully hard to admit to oneself.' He turned to face Cole. Suddenly he felt a great affection for him. 'You see, if I were only eighteen this could be a mad crush that wouldn't last a month. But both you and I have been at the game far too long not to know the difference between falling seriously for a person and a one-night stand.'

Even before Graham had finished speaking Cole began to shake his head.

'But when the difference between your ages is over twenty-five years,' Cole said, 'it's lunatic to allow yourself to fall in love unless the girl's mad for you. And it doesn't sound as if she is. If death is the great leveller, then age is certainly the great divider. The only thing you'll get out of a one-sided affair is sheer hell – no pleasure. And so far you haven't shown any masochistic tendencies. All your other girls have been in the twenty–thirty age-group. Can't you see ? You've suddenly been confronted by the fact that you're middle-aged. You've looked after your figure. You look quite fit. But the cruel truth is that the young have the kind of bodies they don't even have to worry about.'

Graham began playing with his gold ring. His wife had given it to him as a wedding present, and he had ceased to wear it when it had lost all meaning. But he found that he had grown so used to fiddling with it in moments of stress that he had the ring made smaller to fit his little finger.

'Aren't you taking rather a drastic line ?' Graham asked.

'Maybe,' Cole replied. 'But I'm afraid you still think of yourself as Graham Hadley, the brilliant young director, God's gift to starlets. Don't you remember the old slogan – "if Hadley's on the way up, so are you" ? Well, to use your own phrase, you've been at the game a long time, and you should have got this kind of obsession out of your system before now. Let's face it. You have to choose "love" in inverted commas – at a particular level and then stick to it. You know the choice you made, just as I know only too well the choice I made. But I use the words "you have to choose" with this qualification – "unless you want to bitch yourself". The trouble is that you've suddenly discovered that you've been travelling in the wrong direction, and you're trying to jump from one express train to another. If you must have a splendid, romantic, drooling love affair, then for heaven's sake stalk on familiar ground. . . .'

'But it's not as cut and dried as you make out,' Graham interrupted. 'You can't generalize. There aren't any rules unless two people want to make their own. In any case, merely because you've taken a return ticket, it doesn't mean you have to come back. I've told you that I'm in love, and no amount of logic will stop me being in love. If it blows up in my face, then I can only face my unhappiness. You may have common sense on your side, but your reasoning's still negative. After all, what have I got to lose?'

Cole allowed the words to settle before he replied.

'You have a most important thing to lose,' he said, 'and that is your peace of mind, no matter how great or small you reckon it. And with the loss of your peace of mind will go your work and your appreciation of everything else you've built up.'

Graham stared out at the damp pavement.

'I'll just have to risk it,' he said. 'If it results in misery, you'll be able to say "I told you so".'

'It'll be no consolation,' Cole said as the car drew up outside the house in Upper Grosvenor Street.

'Look,' Graham said as he crossed the living-room and handed Cole his drink. 'Let's assume I'm not taking your advice. Let's assume I'm going straight ahead and trying to make something of it. What's my next move?'

'Go on phoning until you get her,' Cole replied. 'She can only tell you to go to hell.'

'Right.'

Graham crossed to the rosewood desk and dialled the number he knew almost as well as his own. The bell rang eleven times before the receiver was lifted the other end.

'Hullo?' He knew at once that it was not Vicky who had answered. Though the voice was young it was hard and precise and held a trace of elocution classes.

'Could I speak to Miss Vicky Tollard?' he asked.

'Who's that speaking?'

'Graham Hadley.'

There was a pause. As a director, he was pleased with the

casual sound of his own voice, but he was dismayed by the obvious falsity of the hesitant reply.

'I'm afraid Vicky Tollard's not here this evening,' the prim voice said. 'I rather think she's down in the country visiting her parents.'

'Could you be very kind and tell her that I called,' Graham said quietly.

'I can tell her when she comes back.'

'Thank you so much. Good evening.'

Graham let the receiver drop on to the cradle and turned to Cole.

'Did you hear that?'

'Most of it.'

'The girl who answered the phone is the girl Vicky shares the flat with. Her name's Muriel. And she was lying. I'm certain of it. Vicky was in the room with her. I could sense it. I'm sure she was there.'

'Then obviously young Vicky Tollard just doesn't want to know,' Cole said. 'So what do you do now?'

Graham poured out two more drinks.

'I'll tell you exactly what I do now,' he said. 'I'm going round to Vicky's flat, and I'm going this very minute.'

'What will you do if she won't let you in? Batter the door down?'

'I'll play it by ear,' Graham said. 'Should we meet at the Hermitage in about an hour's time?'

'By all means. And which should I bring along – a doctor or a solicitor? Or do you think you'll need both?'

Graham caught a glimpse of his taut face in the looking-glass and tried to smile.

'Help yourself to more drinks, won't you?'

'Not another drop. One of us had better keep sober, and it doesn't look as if it'll be you.'

Graham crossed to the chimney-piece and picked up his garage keys, then turned.

'Why don't you tell me that I'm acting like an idiot?' he asked.

Cole lay back placidly on the sofa.

'Because it would have no more effect than a mosquito biting a rhinoceros.'

Graham put the keys in his pocket, gulped down his drink and moved to the door.

'Wish me luck,' he said.

'Oh, I do,' Cole replied. 'Luck, and a faint instinct of self-preservation – combined perhaps with just a tiny grain of common sense.'

6

ONCE he had reached the Earl's Court Road, Graham
stopped the Bentley and examined a street map. Now that
he was on his way he felt calm, almost confident. He discovered that the road in which Vicky lived was next to a
square that he knew, but because of a labyrinth of one-way
streets it was several minutes before he drew up outside a
shabby four-storeyed Victorian house distinguished from
the grimy neighbouring houses by the fact that it had been
painted within the last ten years. Projecting from a
mottled plaque on the right of the door was an array of
old-fashioned bell-knobs of a type seldom used and rarely
connected. Some were identified by cards or slips of paper,
but he looked for the name 'Tollard' in vain. On the as-
sumption that the caretaker would live in the basement he
pulled the lowest bell.

He waited for a long time. Presently, through the frosted
glass of the upper panel of the door he saw a shadow advancing towards him along the dimly-lit hallway. The door
slowly opened and a fat man of about sixty with a pallid
unshaven face peered at him through gold-rimmed spectacles, carefully looking him up and down as if he were
about to measure him for a suit. Then the man nodded his
head several times in approval.

'So glad you could come,' he whispered and put a nervous hand on Graham's arm and edged him into the narrow
hall, closing the door hastily behind them. Away from the
publicity of the street the man relaxed and appeared even
more obese. He was wearing a grubby shirt, crumpled from

the spin-drier of a laundrette, and it hung outside trousers
that could no longer be fastened at the waist.

'You must appreciate that this sort of transaction must
be arranged discreetly,' he said in a quiet, hoarse voice. He
was short-winded and seemed to speak only in theatrical
asides. Graham stared in bewilderment.

'I think there's some . . .'

But the man was not listening, and the stage whispers
were continuing without pause.

'I'd ask you down to my flat, but there's someone there.
And I always believe in complete discretion, as you'll
appreciate. Now I think that Mrs Thompson . . . did she
say Thompson or Timpson ? . . . I think she had told you
that my fee will be thirty-five guineas. Did she tell you
that ?'

By now Graham understood.

'I'm actually trying to find the caretaker,' he said.

A look of fear and hostility came into the man's eyes.

'Then you've not come . . .' The sentence expired on his
lips as he ran out of breath.

'No,' Graham said, 'I haven't.'

'But you rang the bell of my flat, and the caretaker lives
at the top of the building. I was expecting . . .'

'I'm sorry,' Graham said. 'I'm the wrong man. I'm not
looking for a surgeon. But perhaps you could be very kind
and help me. Do you happen to know which floor a Miss
Tollard's flat is on ? It's not marked on the board outside.'

'Is she the girl with long fair hair and a friend who's a
hospital nurse ?'

'That's correct.'

'Then you must go up to the fourth floor, and I think
you'll find it's the flat on the left.'

'Thanks so much.'

The man smirked at him ingratiatingly.

'Not at all. It's a pleasure.' He stood poised for a moment not knowing quite how much he could say. 'And just one thing . . . I'm sure you appreciate that the operation would, of course, have been a strictly legal one.'

'Of course,' Graham replied solemnly.

'Good night,' the man said and scuttled away rapidly down the passage and popped like a sand-crab through a door leading to the dark basement.

The uncarpeted staircase was lit only by the naked lamp-bulb that hung on a worn flex from the ceiling of the desolate hall and by a faint glow from above. Graham gripped the banister tightly and made himself count the number of stairs to avoid thinking about the confrontation that lay immediately ahead. A sickly smell of cabbage pervaded the landing on the first floor. The second landing was odourless and silent. But on the third floor, from the flat to the right came the strident noise of a television programme, over-laying the sound of Mozart's clarinet quintet that seemed to be wafting through the canary-coloured door of the flat opposite. The seventy-sixth stair brought Graham to the fourth floor, and he approached the flat on his left. The door was made of heavy wood and stained dark with age. On it, a highly-polished brass door-handle shone conspicuously like the light of a fishing-smack on a dark sea. Graham pressed the bell which was embedded into the wall and waited. Suddenly the landing was filled with a shaft of light as the door was flung open, and Simon Tasker appeared on the threshold and stood motionless, staring at Graham, his tall figure now blocking the light as if, Graham thought, he were a barricade to prevent any part of Vicky escaping from the flat.

'Good evening,' Simon said, without moving.

Graham had prepared no speech to make to Vicky if she opened the door, so his mind was uninhibited and he was able to think quickly. He gave the young man an off-hand yet friendly smile.

'Hullo,' he said, infusing a warmth into his voice. 'Your godmother told me that I might find you here.'

Simon scowled and shifted his weight uneasily.

'Do you remember the promise I made at her party the other night?' Graham continued smoothly.

'What promise?'

The young man was less hostile now and the stare was no longer sullen.

'I promised I'd try to help you find a part in a film. Well, I happened to run into Larry Bates this afternoon, and he's quite a friend of mine. He's shooting a film in Venice, and I think I've got you a part in it.'

Like all good lies Graham's invention had a basis of truth. In the studio that morning Larry Bates had mentioned his Venetian epic, and Graham knew he could get the young man a part in it in exchange for promising to give one of Larry's nymphets a walk-on part in his next production.

'What kind of a part?' the young man asked. His casual voice failed to hide his eagerness.

'Larry didn't specify,' Graham said. He was lying fluently now. 'I told him how impressed I'd been by you. I described you as best I could, and I could see that he was definitely interested. In fact he wants you to go down to the studios for an audition this very Wednesday.'

For the first time the young man smiled.

'I don't know how to thank you,' he said.

'That's all right,' Graham said, and as he spoke he decided that he must take a risk. He turned very slowly as if to leave, but in his gesture there was a hint of reluctance, a subtly implied promise that if he stayed he could give Simon more information about the film or more help in his

63

career. Half-way through his performance, acting as if the camera were on him in close-up, Graham paused and let his head move round so that his eyes rested on the young man with an expression of concern.

'Do you have to go?' Simon said.

Graham was silent. The trick had worked. He had always maintained that a good director must be able to act better than his stars. He widened his eyes a little and smiled shyly. He was playing his role so intensely that his mind had switched back to the studio, and he could almost feel the heat of the arc lamps.

'Won't you stay and have a drink?' Simon asked.

In turn, Graham registered surprise, a slight hesitancy, and pleasure.

'Thanks,' he said. 'I'd love to.'

Simon abandoned his position as gate-keeper and stood aside.

'Come along in,' he said.

Graham followed him across a dingy hallway. Simon opened a door at the far end that led into the living-room.

'I've asked Mr Hadley to come in for a drink,' he announced defiantly. Then he turned and ushered Graham into the room. Vicky was sprawling on the sofa. Her eyes were fixed on the doorway, and he saw her stiffen and glance towards the girl in nurse's uniform who was sitting beside her.

'I think you've met Vicky,' Simon said with an awkward wave of his hand. 'But I don't think you've met Miss Craig.'

'How do you do,' Graham said pleasantly.

The uniformed girl who was evidently the virtuous Muriel nodded her head and glowered. Graham hoped that his performance of a nonchalant director was convincing the two girls. They were both watching him in the impersonal way they might have watched a window-dresser from the pavement. His eyes moved round the room, noting the cheap grey cord carpet, the tubular chairs with woven plastic seats, uncomfortable copies of a wicker chair, the convertible divan in the corner and the hideous lampshades. All of them proclaimed not so much the impermanence of the furnishings as the transiency of the tenants. It was impossible, he realized, to impose any personality on a furnished flat like this. His glance flickered towards Vicky who was staring with rapt attention at a gilt mirror on the wall opposite. She was wearing a close-fitting jacket of white brocade and looked as if she were dressed to go out to a party.

The silence now seemed to hang over the room like a mist. Simon broke the strain.

'Mr Hadley thinks he may have got me a part in a film,' he said. 'Larry Bates is making the film in Venice.'

Standing nervously in front of the two girls with his feet apart, Simon reminded Graham of a schoolboy explaining to the headmaster how he came to break a window.

'I have to go down to the studios for an audition this Wednesday,' Simon continued.

'Have you now?' the girl who must be Muriel said without interest. As soon as she spoke Graham recognized the cultivated voice he had heard on the telephone. From Vicky's casual references to her, Graham had imagined Muriel as a lanky, long-nose girl with apple cheeks and mouse-coloured hair. But in fact she was small and very slim with sharp features, dark hair, and a dark, almost swarthy complexion. Her close-set eyes gleamed with intelligence, and Graham felt she had the power to be dangerous.

'I'm sure it must be quite lovely in Venice at this time of

year,' Muriel continued in the same flat tone. 'And I'm sure you'll look quite perfect on the Piazza San Marco – particularly by moonlight.'

Graham noticed that she avoided looking at Simon while she spoke and her hands were restless.

'I'm longing for it,' Simon announced firmly.

Graham decided that the moment had come to assert himself unobtrusively. He had noticed an oil-painting above the bleak mantelpiece. It was a seascape – early eighteenth-century and possibly Flemish. It looked out of place in the tawdry room. He crossed over and examined the painting closely.

'It's an enchanting picture,' he said quietly.

Vicky spoke for the first time.

'It comes from Larkin,' she said in a cold voice.

'From larking?' he asked.

'Larkin without a "g",' Vicky replied flatly. 'It's the name of our house in the country.'

Muriel rose abruptly from the sofa.

'I have to be off to hospital,' she announced, moving swiftly towards the door.

'I hope we shall meet again,' Graham said as she passed him.

'I dare say,' Muriel replied. She was unsure of herself and avoided his eyes, but from her disposition he had the impression of an obstinate loyalty to Vicky.

'Good night all,' Muriel cried out from the hall, and the door slammed behind her.

Simon put his hand on the back of one of the tubular chairs. He was uncertain what move to make next. He glanced towards Vicky for guidance, but her eyes were fixed on the cigarette she was holding between her thumb and index finger.

'This isn't my flat,' Simon said, turning back to Graham.

'But I sometimes bring in a bottle, so I can pretend I'm a part-host. So what can I get you to drink?'

'I'll have a whisky if I may.'

'What about you, Vicky?' Simon asked.

Vicky stared intently at the long ash at the end of her cigarette.

'Nothing for me, thanks,' she said.

Simon crossed to a cracked mahogany cupboard and took out a bottle of whisky, a siphon and two glasses.

'Are you sure I can't get you anything, Vicky?' he asked.

'Very sure.'

Graham decided that if Simon was the reason that Vicky no longer wished to see him he had little need to worry unless Simon was deeply in love with her or supremely virtuous, and he seemed to be neither. And if, knowing Graham's reputation, Simon had warned her against him the young man could now be relied on to change his attitude, leaving the ground clear for Graham. Simon handed him his drink. Graham smiled at him encouragingly and for a moment their eyes met.

'If you'll give me your phone number,' Graham told him, 'I'll get Larry's secretary to ring you first thing in the morning.'

'Thanks,' Simon said. 'I really am grateful.'

As he spoke Simon's eyes moved away from Graham's face and veered for an instant towards Vicky, and at once Graham knew that the young man was aware that his efforts to get him a film part were not wholly altruistic. Graham now saw his next step clearly, but when he began to speak his voice sounded to him like an inexperienced barrister thinking out loud before the Bench.

'I've just had an idea,' Graham said. 'Why don't you both come and join me for dinner?'

The wafer of cigarette-ash trembled and fell to dust on

the carpet. Vicky blew away the lingering particles of ash and the tip of her cigarette glowed red. She still gazed down at it.

'I'm dining with an old friend of mine – Cole Edwards,' he continued. 'He's a script-writer. You may have heard of him. He's working on this film we're going to make in Morocco based on the life of Abdel Krim. He's a charmer. So please do come, both of you.'

'Marvellous,' Simon said. 'I'd love to.'

Vicky lifted her head and looked at Graham steadily. 'I'm feeling rather tired,' she said. 'I don't think I'll come.'

'But you were all set to go out to some party,' Simon protested.

Graham wondered if the remark sprang from innocence or a new-found loyalty to him.

'In that case,' he was about to say. But then Cole's words came back to him. 'I suppose there is the possibility,' Cole's voice said in his ear, 'that she's just not interested.' And if Cole were right, he couldn't plead with her and retain his self-respect. Yet he had to make some effort to persuade her to change her mind.

'It'll be an early evening, I promise you,' he said. 'Cole and I have a conference at the studios at nine – which means getting up at seven.'

'Please come,' Simon said. 'I'd like to meet Cole Edwards, but I can't very well leave you alone.'

'I don't see why not. I've dined alone before now.'

Simon strode across to the sofa, took hold of Vicky's arms and pulled her to her feet.

'Upsadaisy like a good girl,' he said cheerfully. 'You know that if you're left by yourself you'll only open a tin of sardines and mope.'

Then he gazed at her forlorn face and bent down and kissed her forehead. The action was so spontaneous that it gave Graham a glimpse into the intimacy of their relationship, and he felt a stab of jealousy as he saw Vicky's lips slowly widen into a smile as she stared up at Simon who was grinning at her affectionately.

'All right,' Vicky said, 'I'll come.'

7

GRAHAM felt exhausted but elated when he let himself into his flat towards midnight: judged by any standards the evening had been a success. Knowing that Vicky did not enjoy the Hermitage he had paused there briefly to collect Cole and he had then taken the three of them to a pleasantly informal restaurant off Bruton Street. The tables were set well apart so one did not have to worry about neighbours, the food was excellent, and there was a small dance-floor at the far end of the room. From the moment they met, Cole had set out to charm Graham's two young guests and he had not failed. He had addressed most of his remarks to Simon who was a little overawed, while discreetly playing up to Vicky who was not, and Graham could see they were both fascinated by his mixture of worldly cynicism and pure childishness.

'I do see just what you mean,' Cole said to Graham after they had eaten and Vicky and Simon were dancing together. 'I think she's a knock-out. She's got the kind of wistful look I find so madly appealing. One feels she's been lost in a dark maze for years and she's desperately longing to find her way out. . . . You can see how sentimental a combination of youth and Krug makes me. . . . And she's got one of the most beautifully made bodies I've seen for ages. In fact, I don't mind telling you that if I were a few years younger I'd pop arsenic into your coffee this very night.'

'So you don't think I'm making a mistake?'

'My dear Graham, of course you're making a mistake. A whacking great catastrophic mistake that will probably ruin you. But when I saw the expression of yearning in those eyes I realized there was nothing to be done about it.'

'Did you know she wore contact lenses?' Graham asked, blandly.

'I don't believe you.'

'She does. They just cover the iris.'

'Do you think I should try them?' Cole asked, taking off his spectacles and giving Graham a wide toothy grin. Then he looked at himself in the mirrored wall behind them and sighed. 'No, perhaps not. Besides, I like my glasses. I feel I can withdraw behind my thick lenses like an old turtle into its shell. And I may say that I needed the protection of my spectacles when I first clapped eyes on Miss Tollard – not that I really care. Like Melba, I've retired from my triumphs, and like Melba I should have retired at least twenty years sooner.'

Graham smiled.

'But I thought . . .'

'Yes. And you thought right. A merry little frolic once a fortnight. But nothing serious any longer. No love for yours truly. His sense of self-protection is far too well developed – unlike yours,' Cole added as Vicky and Simon rejoined their table.

At eleven Cole had announced that he must leave.

'I live in the wilds of St John's Wood,' he said. 'And I need at least seven hours' beauty sleep.'

Graham remembered his promise to Vicky and called for the bill.

71

'Good night, children,' Cole said as they stood outside the restaurant and the commissionaire brought round a taxi. 'Don't lead Graham astray.'

'We won't,' Simon promised.

Cole leaned out of the taxi window.

'And don't let him stay up all night and ruin his health,' he said. 'He's a valuable property is Graham. He's the only director we've got on this picture – so far,' he called out as the taxi moved away.

'Does he always have to have the last word?' Vicky asked.

'Always,' Graham assured her as they walked towards his black Bentley that was parked opposite. 'And now what would you like to do?' he asked, opening the door for Vicky. 'Shall we move on to some club or would you rather go home?'

'Home, I think, for me,' Vicky said.

'Could you drop me on the way?' Simon asked. 'I live in a mews in Kinnerton Street. So it'd be fine if you could drop me off at the top of Wilton Crescent.'

Simon was learning fast.

'If you don't mind, I shan't ask you up for a night-cap,' Vicky said, gazing fixedly at the road ahead.

They had said good night to Simon and were now driving along the Brompton Road. Graham was silent.

'Are you annoyed?' Vicky had asked.

'No.'

'Then why are you so quiet?'

'Is it the next turning to the left?'

'Yes. And then it's first right,' Vicky replied. 'But you *are* annoyed, aren't you?'

'I'm not,' Graham said. 'But I'd like to ask you a question.'

'Then ask it – though I don't promise to answer.'

'Why didn't you turn up last night?'

'I'm sorry,' Vicky said in a casual voice. 'It's not the first on the right. It's the *second* on the right.'

'Why didn't you turn up?'

Vicky took a packet of cigarettes and a lighter from her bag.

'Can I light you a cigarette?' she asked.

'Please.'

She put two cigarettes into her mouth, lit them both expertly, took out one of them and handed it to Graham with a ceremonious wave of her hand. Perhaps it was a ritual that she performed for Simon.

'Are you going to answer my question?' he asked.

She pulled out the ashtray beneath the dashboard.

'I'll try to,' she said. 'But it's not going to be easy. You see, in fact there were really two reasons.'

She tapped the ashtray with her cigarette.

'The first reason was Simon. I knew he was very fond of me, and I didn't want to make him unhappy. But I needn't have worried myself about him.'

'What makes you say that?'

Vicky turned her head and looked at him.

'Well, I may be young,' she said, 'but I'm not a fool. And I saw what was going on behind the scenes tonight. Mind you, I don't blame him. I'm sure I'd have done the same myself. But he did make it perfectly clear that his career mattered to him more than I did. Or don't you agree?'

'What was the second reason?' Graham asked.

'It's the fourth house past that lamp-post on the left.'

'I know,' Graham said. 'I shan't forget the number.'

73

He drew up the car outside the peeling columns of the Victorian porch.

'The second reason?' he asked.

'That's the hardest one to explain. You see, the second reason was *you*.'

'How so?'

'Well, you obviously wanted to take it all seriously. I mean, you didn't want just a casual relationship, did you?'

'That's true.'

'So I didn't want to hurt you. It's as simple as that. . . . Graham, please try to understand me. I don't *want* people to fall in love with me. I don't *want* people to try to possess me. I'm young and I want to enjoy myself while I can. I want to go out with who I like, and when I like – without feeling that I'm hurting someone's feelings. I'm not ready to settle down yet – not even with a person as young and attractive as Simon. I enjoy having friends and I enjoy having affairs, but I don't want to tie myself down to anyone for good. I'm sure I'll want that kind of solid relationship one day. But not just yet.'

The night was warm and still, and the street seemed very quiet. From far off they could hear the siren of a barge on the Thames. It sounded reproachful, as if reminding him of a facet of life that was harder than his own.

'Listen, Vicky,' Graham said. 'Supposing I were to accept your terms? Supposing I were to enter into this knowing that it might never be serious and might never be permanent, then you need never feel guilty whatever happens, need you?'

A car stopped at the far end of the street, and they heard its door open and shut.

'I did warn you in my letter, didn't I?' she said.

'You did.'

Vicky stubbed out her cigarette.

74

'If you're really prepared to be satisfied with the little I've got to offer you,' she said, 'then so far as I'm concerned – I'd love us to meet again. And let's see how it all pans out.'

'How about tomorrow night then?' he said. 'It's the opening of the new Grantley play at the Comedy Theatre. Will you come with me?'

'That's fine.'

'Shall I collect you?'

'No. I'll meet you at the theatre.'

He leaned across and kissed her on the forehead.

'Bless you,' he said. 'See you about seven-forty-five. The curtain goes up at eight.'

He got out and opened the door for her.

'Good night, Graham. And thanks for another splendid evening.'

'Let's hope there'll be more,' he said with a smile.

And there would be more, he thought, as he walked down the corridor of his flat towards his bedroom, many more. And the very next of them would start within twenty-four hours.

8

VICKY moved away from the mirror, picked up her glass of champagne from the marble-topped table, and came back to sit down beside him on the sofa.

'Is it in position?' Graham asked.

'Look into my eyes,' Vicky said. 'Do you notice anything?'

'They're blue and they're quite beautiful.'

'Do you notice anything different from last night?'

'They seem brighter, but perhaps that's the light.'

'Well, actually it's not. You see, the reason they look bright blue is that I've got in my new contact lenses and they're tinted. Last night I was wearing the natural ones.'

Graham leaned over and kissed her.

'Vicky,' he said, 'you're wonderful.'

'Now you're laughing at me,' she said.

He stood up and fetched the bottle of champagne and filled their two glasses.

'I wish I were eighteen and madly attractive,' he said. 'I wish I were young and radiant and so glowing with vitality that you simply couldn't resist me. But as it is – I can only tell you that I love you very much.'

Vicky began fingering the two gold bracelets on her left wrist.

'I'm fond of you, Graham,' she said. 'I'm interested in you and in your life. I'm amused by the places we go to, and I'm fascinated to meet all the celebrities we did tonight. Each time we go out together I like you more. But you know the form. I'm sure I could love you in time. But

76

I could never fall in love with you – because we're not the same age.'

'Does it make so much difference?'

Vicky stopped playing with her bracelets and looked up at him.

'It makes all the difference.'

'But the other night . . .'

'I was quite drunk.'

'But you weren't in the morning.'

Vicky stood up.

'All right,' she said. 'If you want the truth, I enjoyed it. And I enjoyed it the first time. You see, I wasn't too drunk to remember. And the reason is that you know how to excite me. You seem to know instinctively. So it's fine. But when it's all over, I feel somehow that it's wrong.'

'How is it wrong?'

'Like one note of a chord in music can be wrong.'

'Do you feel that because it's true or because you want to believe that age can make a difference?'

'To be honest, I'm not sure. But I have an awful feeling that it's not going to work out.'

Graham moved towards her and took her hand.

'It *will* work out. We can be happy together – I'm certain. So shall we drink to that?'

'If you like,' she said, raising her glass.

'Vicky, give up your job and come and work for me. I think you'd find it all quite interesting.'

'I don't want to be kept.'

'But you wouldn't be.'

'That's what it would come down to in the end.'

He took the empty glass from her hand and put his arms round her.

'You think it won't work, and I'm sure it will,' he said. 'So can't we put it to the test?'

'How can we?'

Her arms were limp at her side.

'When do you get a holiday?'

'Fairly soon, I expect.'

'Cole and I are off to Tangier in a fortnight. We've got to see officials there, and then we move up into the Rif mountains to find locations for this film on Abdel Krim. Why don't you come with us?'

Vicky took his hands and gently detached them from her waist and moved to the far end of the room. When she turned round she was frowning in concentration like a child trying to solve a difficult equation.

'If I do come,' she said, 'I'll pay my own fare, and I'll be going out there because I want a holiday. I'll be going out because I want to have fun. And you know what I mean. Part of the time I shall want to be with people of my own age. So don't . . . so don't expect to have a monopoly.'

Graham laughed.

'The way you put it, I don't quite see what I'm supposed to get out of it.'

Vicky looked at him solemnly.

'You'd always have first call,' she said.

The blatant sincerity of her answer together with its implications at once appalled and thrilled him. And like the slide of a lantern there glided into his mind an image of Vicky lying naked on his bed. At first the picture was blurred but gradually it came into focus and he could see her small breasts and lean thighs and long soft legs. His voice sounded thick as he spoke.

'And can I have first call tonight?'

Vicky hesitated. Then she moved slowly towards him.

78

PART TWO

1

ACROSS the tarmac they saw a lone figure pressed against the railing of the terrace outside the airport restaurant, waving to them. It was Cole, who had already adapted himself to the summer heat of Tangier – for he was wearing a white bush-shirt and a thin pair of lilac shorts.

'I'm a prisoner of the customs,' he called out. 'They've arrested me twice for trying to get on to the air-strip, and they're very strong.'

As he spoke two black-belted officials in grey uniform moved towards him. 'Meet you outside the main hall,' Cole cried as he darted away.

Vicky had felt stifled and ill in the small D.C.3 plane that connected Gibraltar with Tangier, and Graham tried not to be irritated by the inefficiency and delays of the Moroccan customs.

'Don't fret,' Vicky said. 'Cole won't mind waiting.'

'But you're tired and you need to lie down.'

'You mustn't talk as if we were a married couple,' Vicky laughed. She was still pale but her face was trembling with excitement – like a child on a school-treat, Graham thought.

While they were filling in various forms for the Moroccan police-control, Graham noticed a young official eyeing Vicky.

'Your daughter, monsieur?' the young man asked as he stamped Graham's form.

'No,' Graham said.

'Your friend?' the young man asked knowingly. And for the first time Graham could read clearly the message that Cole had tried to spell out to him.

'Yes,' he replied without looking at Vicky.

They collected their luggage and found two porters who followed them through the main hall and out through the swing-doors to the asphalt square in front of the portico where Cole was waiting in the early morning sunshine.

'Thank heavens you've got porters, so I needn't carry a single case,' he said, taking them by the arm and leading them across the car park. 'It's a perfectly hideous apartment, but it'll do – as the duchess said when she poured the Napoleon brandy over the Christmas pudding. And just wait till you see the car I've hired. There! Just *look* at it!'

He pointed towards a very large and old black Chevrolet.

'Doesn't it look exactly like a hearse? But it was the best I could find, and it goes like a bomb. I even drove it here and scared myself to death. However, I expect, Graham, you'd prefer to take over from here on.'

'I certainly would,' Graham said.

They drove along the dusty road that led into the town, passing old women bent double under loads of brushwood, bearded Moors in tattered djellabas sitting sideways on the rumps of their donkeys ('straight out of a Bible epic,' Cole said), past Berber women in white robes and wide-brimmed straw hats that made them look like mushrooms, past outlying villas and filling-stations, until in the distance they saw long rows of white and grey blocks of flats and hotels, some square and others circular like toy bricks, some tall and narrow, clustered thickly on the hillside that led up to the Kasbah. And meanwhile Cole prattled away, selecting at random from the pile of varied information he had managed to glean in less than a week.

'Of course, the most romantic place to bathe is on the

Atlantic beach beyond Cap Spartel, but it's twenty minutes' drive away from town, and the breakers are so huge that they knocked yours truly flat. The terrible thing is that under that pile of scrub-wood we've just passed there's either an old lady or a camel. . . . On the Mediterranean side – so nice being able to choose, isn't it ? – there's the Tangier *plage* itself. Imagine Brighton beach transplanted to Africa, and it gives you some idea. And I may say it's a positive forest of eyes. I felt quite shy . . . but not for long. Any old how, stretching for at least a mile are all those beach bars. And I was sauntering past one of them, holding in my tummy as usual, when who should I see swigging down a Pernod on the wrong side of the bar but Evelyn Roper. You turn left here, Graham. . . . Well, Evelyn's an old dyke from way back. I hadn't seen her for a decade. So I pranced in and found she was running the place. You'll both of you like the bar. With your first Flag Pils you're a friend for life. But the familiarity's not offensive. . . . Now you turn right. . . . The hospitality's strictly personal, but the terms are, of course, strictly cash. Even in Tangier, alas, there's a price on sweetness. . . . And now if you turn left, that's us.'

They drove into a broad, empty road lined at odd intervals with thin, drooping trees and called the Boulevard de Paris. Half-way down the incline they stopped outside a small block of flats. The building had once been painted green, but the colour had faded in the heat of the sun, and the paint was peeling from the mottled walls.

They walked up the stone steps of an echoing staircase and stopped outside the door of a flat on the third floor. Cole rang the bell and then took out a key.

'I expect the Fatima's out shopping as usual,' he said.

He led them along an uncarpeted corridor of a speckled composite material and threw open the double doors that led into a brightly-painted living-room with modern black-leather chairs and light-wood furniture, and a long curved window at the far end.

'Cole, I think you've done wonderfully,' Vicky said.

'So do I,' Graham said in a stage whisper. 'But I'm not saying too much about it in case he asks for a rise.'

He knew his remark was silly and unfunny, but he felt light-headed, for he had reached Tangier, and Vicky was by his side.

'Now come and see the bedrooms,' Cole ordered. 'There are only two, so I've given you the one with the largest bed.'

The rooms were sparsely furnished but they looked clean, and the beds were comfortable.

'There's ice in the fridge and plenty of booze when any-one wants a drink,' Cole said.

'Where shall we have lunch?' Graham asked. 'Here or at some restaurant?'

Cole snapped his fingers.

'I'm sorry, Graham,' he said, 'but I clean forgot. They rang up from the Amalat to ask if you could lunch with the Governor today, and I said I'd ring back to let them know. You're the only one of us invited, but I think you ought to make an appearance.'

'Hell!' Graham said. 'I suppose I should. Or could I ask them to postpone it?'

'You've got to go sooner or later,' Cole said. 'Let me take Vicky down to Evelyn's bar, and we'll lunch there. We can order cold lobster and drink local wine.'

He turned to Vicky. 'Then after lunch you can offer yourself to the waves while I lie flat on my back on the sand and go to sleep. And Graham can join us on the beach as soon as he's finished lunch with the Governor.'

Vicky was standing close to the looking-glass taking out a contact lens.

'Is that all right with you, Vicky?' Graham asked.

'Yes,' she replied vaguely. 'That's all right.'

'Splendid,' Cole said, as he left the room. 'Let's meet for a drink in the living-room about noon.'

'Has it slipped again?' Graham asked.

'No. But I've got to put in a new pair, because I lost one in the 'plane.'

'Why didn't you tell me?'

'I didn't want you to worry. Besides, even if we'd found it, the lens would have been broken, with all those people trampling about. They're so delicate you can even scratch one picking it up.'

'How many pairs have you got left?'

'Only two now. It always makes me furious when I lose one because they cost forty pounds a pair, and I've lost so many that they won't insure me any more.'

'Why don't you wear spectacles? I believe you'd look enchanting.'

'I can never wear spectacles,' Vicky said violently. 'They give me the most terrible inferiority complex.'

Graham went up to her and kissed the back of her head.

'Do you think you'll be happy here?'

'I'm sure I will,' she said, staring at the reflection of his face in the mirror, 'if you'll only stop mussing my hair about.' Then she turned from the glass.

'I love the expression on your face when you're offended,' she said, stroking his forehead. 'It makes you look like a small boy.'

.   .   .   .   .

Graham parked the Chevrolet in front of the Rif Hotel, crossed the dual carriageway, and ran down the steps that led on to the beach. An asphalt path separated the long row of bathing-huts and bars from a vast stretch of flat sand thickly dappled with bodies whose colours ranged from milk-white to chestnut-brown and from sun-burnt scarlet to prune-black. The bar was called La Ronde, Cole had said, and you turned left from the main entrance.

The tall woman on the balcony stopped scolding the wizened Moroccan waiter as he approached.

'You must be Graham Hadley,' she said. 'We were expecting you. How was lunch with the Governor?'

'Sumptuous,' Graham said. 'Ten courses, but nothing stronger than lemonade.'

'That's the form, so I'm told. And what can we get you now? The first drink's on the house. After that it's strictly cash. What will it be? We've got the lot.'

'I'd love a cuba libre.'

'Abdesselem!' she called. 'Now where's he got to?'

The wizened waiter advanced towards them, moving oddly, as if he were treading water.

'Wahad cuba libre,' Evelyn Roper said, speaking like a schoolmistress to a backward child. 'Un cuba libre. Do you understand *cuba libre*? Bacardi, Coca-Cola, slice of lemon, and plenty of ice.'

Abdesselem nodded his head quickly like a clockwork doll, but not a glimmer of understanding showed on his face.

'It's no good,' she said. 'He's full of Kif as usual. When they told me I ought to have a man about the place, I should have trusted my better instinct. I'll have to go and get it myself. I'm simply lost without Susan. But she left in a huff – taking most of the cash with her,' Evelyn explained as she strode away.

The woman must be nearly six feet tall, Graham reckoned. She had a thin face and a long hooked nose, and her grey hair was cut in a fringe that reached the thick dark brows above her deep-set eyes. She might have been a priestess at the temple of Jupiter Ammon.

'That's an attractive girl you've brought out with you,' Evelyn said when she returned with a cuba libre for him and a Pernod for herself. 'She'll have the time of her life out here.'

'Let's hope so.'

'The natives will go crazy for her. They're always wild for blondes. Susan's got very fair hair, and I have to watch her like a lynx. Not that she's really interested. But you can never be too sure.'

Evelyn sank down her Pernod rapidly and wiped her mouth with a paper napkin.

'And now you must excuse me,' she said. 'I have to drive up into town to try to appease the poor girl. When you want to change out of your clothes, Abdesselem's got the key to your cabin – if you ask him five times in your best Arabic. . . . See you later.'

Graham picked his way through little groups of prostrate sun-bathers towards the sea. The sand was so hot that he had to return to the cabin to put on some sandals. The beach was now crowded. Pink-skinned plump tourists wandered along the water's edge surrounded by hordes of dark, almost naked, little boys frisking in and out of the sea. Further inland clusters of Moroccan women, draped in wool, sat exposing a few square inches of their faces to the sun. Husky young men flexed their muscles as they threw a beach-ball around their exclusive ring.

87

Then Graham spotted Cole amongst the shoals of bodies. He was reclining on a turquoise towel, and his wrinkled skin was pleasantly brown. A few feet away from him, lying on the outsize beach-towel that Graham had bought her in London, with her head resting on her hands, was Vicky, and sprawling in the sand around her in their bathing-slips were three young Moroccans whose ages, he guessed, ranged from sixteen to about twenty-four. One of them, the most finely-built of the three and certainly the most handsome, had edged his way on to the border of Vicky's towel and was kneeling beside her. His right hand was stretched out towards Vicky's forearm, but only the tips of three fingers of his hand were touching her skin, as if that small patch of her flesh were a talisman.

As Graham approached Cole looked up, glanced towards the three youths, and grinned at him apologetically.

'It didn't quite work out as I'd planned,' he said wryly.

Vicky turned her head.

'Hullo,' she said, 'did you have a good lunch?'

'Fine.'

He noticed that the young man's fingers did not move – nor did Vicky appear to be at all embarrassed.

'Spread out your towel by mine and come and join us,' she said, raising herself on an elbow. 'And now I must introduce you.'

She looked towards the young man whose fingers had been touching her.

'This is Hamido,' she said.

The young man – he looked about twenty – sprang to his feet and seized Graham's hand. He spoke haltingly and with a distinctly American accent, Graham observed. 'I am pleased to meet you,' he said. Though his body was firmly compact, his limbs were slender and he moved lightly. His golden-brown skin was smooth and hairless, and beneath the coarse mat of jet-black curls that fell around his forehead his light-coloured eyes seemed almost violet.

Vicky pointed towards the largest of the three of them – the one with a pock-marked face, who was probably twenty-four.

'And this is Ibrahim. . . . Am I right?' Vicky asked.

The large one gave a grunt of assent. He was leaning on his left elbow and he raised his right hand in greeting. His huge body was covered with hair, like an ape.

Vicky glanced towards the youngest of them – the slender boy of about sixteen who was sitting cross-legged in the sand playing with a string of glass beads.

'The terrible thing is that I can't remember your name,' she said.

The boy's long eyelashes fluttered like a drowsy butterfly as he grinned at Vicky and said nothing.

'Comment t'appelles-tu?'

'Hassan,' he whispered in a soft, hoarse voice. 'Ai em kelled Hassan.'

'Straight out of Flecker,' Cole said.

Graham had spread out his wrap so that it touched the border of Vicky's towel, and he now opened her beach-bag and took out a bottle of sun-tan lotion.

'If you don't put on some oil in this sun you'll burn,' he said, pouring the lotion on to his hands.

'Lie still,' he ordered and slowly he began to massage the liquid into her skin, sliding his hands over her shoulders and along her arms and down her back. And as his hands moved up and down Vicky's slim body with their rhythmic intimate caress, Graham glanced up at Hamido who had so recently been kneeling beside her. The young man was

89

staring down at them. The smile had left his face. For an instant his eyes met Graham's. Then he turned away quickly towards Ibrahim and the boy Hassan who were lying close to him. He called out something in Arabic, and the two of them rose, laughing, and began wrestling with him in the sand a few yards away, hurling each other to the ground, and bursting into loud, self-conscious laughter. Then, seeing Vicky's lack of interest in their breathless struggles, they began to perform acrobatics that were evidently designed to display their well-developed muscles and virility.

Suddenly Vicky raised herself. Her body was glistening with oil.

'Do go and play somewhere else,' she said. 'You're kicking up the sand, and it gets into my eyes.'

Graham expected Hamido to look offended, but he beamed at her warmly, gave another shout to his friends, and the three of them ran off along the beach.

When their over-enthusiastic laughter had faded away, Graham moved close to Vicky and took her hand and felt her fingers twine with his, and presently he fell asleep. As the afternoon passed by, he was vaguely aware that Vicky had gone off to have a swim, and dimly he was conscious of the return of the three young Moroccans. Through half-opened eyes he saw they were now clustered round Cole's towel, and as he dozed he could hear fragments of their conversation.

'Ibrahim is twenty-six years of age.' He recognized Hamido's American accent. 'He is the oldest of us and he is the biggest. We call him the donkey, but I am much stronger than him.'

'I dare say,' Cole said. 'Those shoulders and all those rippling muscles and that glabrous chest – no wonder Ibrahim stares at you so jealously. . . . Can he understand a word I say? I do hope not. . . . And tell me, Hamido, you beautiful child of nature, what do they call *you*?'

'How you say in English a young horse?'

'Just like that I reckon. And what do you call your wicked-looking young Hassan?'

'The little fish.'

'Leetlle feesh,' Hassan whispered proudly.

'But tell me, Hamido, how come you speak English so well?'

'I have an American friend.'

'Ah, now we're getting places. And how old is your friend?'

'I don't know. She is not old.'

'What do you do? What's your job?'

There was a grunt that sounded as if it came from Ibrahim.

'I work sometimes in a garage,' Hamido's voice said. 'I am mechanic.'

'Do you enjoy it?'

'No. Because it is dirty work. And I do not like to have my neck and my arms and all my body dirty. Because then when I finish work I must go back to where I live and spend much time washing myself. . . .'

At about that moment Graham must have dozed off again, for he could remember nothing more of the conversation. When he awoke the sun was low in the sky, and Cole was snoring softly. He raised himself and saw Vicky and Hamido coming out of the sea and walking towards him. He noticed that they never even glanced at each other, and both of them were silent.

'Hullo,' Vicky said as he handed her the towel. 'You've been asleep quite a while. Don't you think it's time we went back?'

'Yes, I do,' Cole said, now wide awake. 'I'm burnt to a cinder.'

'Come on then,' Graham said, picking up Vicky's beach-bag.

He noticed that Vicky was quiet as they sauntered across the beach to the row of brightly-painted bathing-cabins adjoining Evelyn's bar. She seemed preoccupied.

When he came out on to the terrace, he saw that the door of Vicky's cabin was still closed. Hamido was standing on the asphalt path leaning against the white wall of the restaurant. He was now wearing a pillar-box-red T-shirt above his swimming-shorts. He grinned at Graham nervously, but made no move to come into the bar.

'Will you have a drink?' Graham felt obliged to ask.

'Thank you. I would like one.'

'Then come along in.'

Hamido jumped over the low wall and sat down at the table opposite Graham.

'What will you have?' Graham asked as the shrivelled waiter trod his way cautiously towards them.

'An orange drink, please.'

'And a cuba libre, please, Abdesselem,' Graham said, pleased that he had remembered the waiter's name.

Abdesselem bowed reverently to Graham and gave a short sniff as he passed Hamido's chair, leaving them in silence. Graham searched for something to say.

'Do your family live in Tangier?' he asked after a while.

Hamido was playing with a straw that had been left on the damp table, twisting it between his blunt fingers.

'No,' he said. 'My father is dead. But my mother and my brother live in Fez.'

92

He began to fold the straw into small sections.

'My brother drives a taxi,' he added.

'Is he older or younger than you?'

'Seven years older.'

His eyes were following a large white car that was moving along the jetty to the left of the beach. As Abdesselem lowered their glasses hesitantly on to the table, Cole appeared from his cabin and staggered towards them, one arm outstretched, the other clutching at his throat, miming a ham-actor dying of thirst. Hamido stared at him in wide-eyed astonishment, then broke into loud laughter.

'Thank heavens there's one appreciative member of my audience,' Cole said as he joined them at the table. 'And I'll have a large gin-and-tonic please, Abdesselem.'

Graham was watching Hamido's broad hand as it rested on the table. When he saw the fingers suddenly curl inwards he knew without turning that Vicky had come out of her cabin.

'What can I get you?' Cole called out.

'Nothing, thanks,' Vicky said. 'Shall we go?'

'Have a heart,' Graham said. 'Let us have our drinks.'

Vicky sat down on the balcony-rail, apparently unaware that Hamido's eyes were fixed on her.

'I didn't want to hurry you,' she said. 'But I've got sand in my eye and a headache from that inoculation I was made to have.'

'But apart from angina pectoris she's feeling fine,' Cole said. Hamido took out a crushed packet of cigarettes and handed them round.

'You like Moroccan cigarettes?' he asked, gazing at Vicky.

'Very much,' she replied as he struck a match and held it out for her.

'I like American more,' Hamido said. 'But they cost too much money.'

'How much do these cost?'

'One dirham a packet.'

Vicky was carefully examining the lines of his face.

'And American cigarettes?'

'Three times as much.'

Cole leaned across to Graham.

'Scintillating dialogue,' he whispered, gulping his drink which had just arrived. 'I'm green with envy.'

'They're young,' Graham said as he paid Abdesselem. He was determined to remain unruffled and indulgent.

'But sometimes they are smuggled in,' Hamido continued, his eyes never leaving Vicky's face. 'And then they are cheaper.'

'Is there much smuggling?'

'Very much.'

Cole finished his glass, and Graham stood up.

'So shall we go home?'

'Let's,' Vicky said.

Hamido escorted them along the asphalt path and walked across the road with them to the Chevrolet. As Graham put the car in gear, Hamido lifted his right hand and waved to them. His eyes were fastened on Vicky. At the Hotel Miramar Graham turned left into the road leading to the centre of town. He glanced back. The boy was standing in the road, gazing after the car with his arm still raised.

Their Fatima – the name used by all Europeans in Morocco for their maidservant – had appeared that evening swathed in the anonymity of the concealing haik of purdah. Once she had shut the door behind her and felt herself secure from the eyes of male Moroccans, she had unswathed herself and appeared as a round-faced, smiling woman of fifty. She had prepared a meal of prawns and thin swordfish steaks.

After dinner, Cole lay stretched out on the black-leather sofa reading through the final treatment of Abdel Krim and Graham was pretending to be absorbed by the *Journal de Maroc*, while his mind made an inventory of Vicky's behaviour since their arrival in Tangier some twelve hours ago. First item: attitude towards him colder. Second item: talking more to Cole than to him. Third and most important item: undisguised interest in Hamido. His built-in computer ticked on remorselessly, when suddenly he heard a noise that reminded him of tanks rumbling over a cobbled street. Cole raised his eyes from the typescript.

'That will be Vicky running herself a bath,' he explained. 'When I first turned on the hot tap in this flat I thought I was in for an earthquake. But it's only the heating system.'

A few minutes later Vicky strode into the living-room in a bath-robe.

'I've done it,' she announced. 'I've dropped my bottle of eye lotion down the loo, and I've cracked the bowl.'

Cole glanced at her distraught face.

'That'll take all my diplomatic charm with our French landlady below,' he said.

Vicky turned towards Graham. She looked pathetic, he thought, with her wet hair framing her strained face.

'I'm sorry, Graham.'

He crossed and put his arm round her.

'Forget it,' he said. 'After all, what's a lavatory between friends?'

They walked arm-in-arm down the corridor to their bedroom which was now littered with Vicky's clothes. When they had turned out the lights, they could see the star-pierced sky framed by the half-open shutter. Before he fell asleep he was conscious of the smoothness of her skin and the feel of her damp hair against his shoulder.

2

THE dust-bin at the corner of the restaurant's balcony was heaped with empty bottles and broken glasses.

'Susan condescended to come down to the bar last night,' Evelyn explained. 'So we had a bit of a party. But you must have been round the town yourself. You look worn out.'

'I am,' Graham said. 'I've spent the whole morning with Moroccan officials. Need I say more?'

'What have you done with Cole? Gagged him?'

'He said he'd go for a stroll.'

'Let's hope he left his wallet behind. . . . Cuba libre?'

'Thanks,' Graham said. 'By the way, have you seen Vicky anywhere around? I couldn't find her on the beach.'

'She's on the sun-terrace up on the roof. And I may tell you that she's not alone. That young Moroccan boy they call Hamido – he's with her, looking as if he were going to eat her. Perhaps we'd better join them.'

'Don't worry,' Graham said lightly. 'Vicky knows how to look after herself.'

Evelyn glanced at him slyly.

'That's just what I'm afraid of,' she said.

Graham laughed and followed her up the steep flight of stairs that led to the terrace. The sun was beating down on the white concrete, and it was almost unbearably hot. On a wide canvas-covered mattress at the far end, Vicky and Hamido in their swimming-slips were lying asleep side by side, about a foot apart, with lines of sweat running down their motionless bodies, as if they were wax figures melting in the heat.

Evelyn clapped her hands.

'Wake up,' she said. 'You've got visitors.'

Vicky turned round, and Hamido scrambled to his feet.

'I was expecting you hours ago,' Vicky said to Graham. 'Where have you been?'

'Trying to get facilities for our location,' Graham said, stretching his lips into a pleasant smile. 'Good afternoon, Hamido.'

The boy was brushing the sweat off his chest with his large hands.

'Good afternoon,' he muttered.

Evelyn pointed her long nose towards Hamido like a retriever.

'I saw your two friends waiting for you downstairs,' she said. 'Hadn't you better go and join them?'

Hamido shuffled his feet awkwardly and stared at the floor.

'Yes,' he said. 'I join them.' And with his eyes still lowered he moved away. But at the top of the staircase he paused and flung back his head and spoke to Vicky.

'Then good-bye,' he said.

'See you later, Hamido,' Vicky said. 'Be good.'

The boy raised his hand in farewell and walked quickly down the stairs without looking back.

'If I were you,' Evelyn said to Vicky, 'I wouldn't get too friendly with the natives. It can land you in terrible trouble.'

'What kind of trouble?'

'Well, firstly, they don't know the meaning of the word "honesty". A boy like Hamido would think nothing of pinching those two bracelets of yours.'

'And secondly?' Vicky asked. Her lips were stiff.

98

'Secondly, they can get quite nasty – especially when there's a gang of them together.'

'I don't think you can lump them all together like that in one undesirable category,' Vicky said. 'And you're obviously biased since you call them natives.'

Evelyn bristled. 'Well, I should tell you that there was an American girl here last year who had the same attitude as you have, and she landed in hospital for two months. I saw her after they'd finished with her.'

Graham decided to intervene.

'Speaking of bracelets,' he said, touching the thick gold band on Evelyn's muscular arm. 'Where did you get that one? It's beautiful.'

'Here in Tangier. The Jews in the Medina are wonderful craftsmen. You ought to take Vicky to see their work.'

Her remark was obviously intended as an apology for her previous brusqueness.

'Can I see it?' Vicky asked.

Evelyn unfastened the clasp and handed the bracelet to her.

'It's lovely,' Vicky said. 'And what a curious design.'

'That's a sentence in Arabic letters.'

'What does it say?'

'Would you like me to read it to you?'

'Please.'

'Well it reads, "Evelyn Roper is an interfering old cow and should get her friends a drink in the bar".'

'So if I bought one, mine would read, "Vicky Tollard R.I.P. – Ravished In Public",' Vicky said as they walked down the stairs.

'"And the bracelet was donated by an ageing friend",' Graham added.

'No, Graham,' Vicky said. 'I don't want you to buy me

one. I'll cable home for some money and buy myself a couple.'

'Well, if you do,' Evelyn said, 'I wouldn't wear them if you're out by yourself on a dark night.'

They sat in the living-room of the flat drinking orange juice from the full jug that the Fatima had left in the refrigerator.

'Why won't you let me buy those bracelets?' Graham asked.

'Because my parents give me an allowance, and anyhow I'm being paid by the firm for these three weeks.'

'That doesn't stop me buying you two bracelets.'

'But I'd rather you didn't.'

'Why?'

'Perhaps it's because I don't want to be dependent on you.' Vicky took a small brown bottle from her bag and unscrewed the eye-dropper that was fixed in the top of it. 'Where's Cole?'

'Fast asleep. I've just been along to his room.'

Vicky tilted back her head and began squeezing out drops of lotion into her eyes.

'It's this wretched sand getting into them,' she said, mopping her cheeks with a handkerchief. 'What are we doing tonight?'

'Martin Ford's giving a party, and we've all three been invited.'

'Who's Martin Ford?'

'He used to be an impresario. He'd put on anything from *War and Peace* on ice to *Charley's Aunt* adapted for Grand Opera. Then an aunt died and left him a fortune, and he produced an epic in six acts that he'd written himself on

100

the life of Nero. It was called *The Emperor*, and it ran for three nights, so he retired in disgust, bought himself a house here in the Kasbah, transplanted some of the décor, and cast himself as Nero, and plays the rôle – or so I'm told – day in, day out.'

'What time is the party?'

'It starts at nine-thirty, so I thought we could eat at the Parade Restaurant first.'

Vicky stretched out her arm and put it behind Graham's neck on the back of the sofa.

'I shall have to leave at eleven,' she said.

'Why?'

'I've arranged to meet Hamido at the Coconut Bar.'

Graham could feel the muscles of his face tightening.

'Don't you think you might at least tell me the arrangements you make?'

Vicky regarded him bleakly. 'I might ask the same thing. If only you'd told me about the party, I wouldn't have made any plans.'

Graham breathed out quickly. 'Plans! My dear Vicky, I think you ought to see things in proportion.'

Vicky stood up.

'I know just what the evening will be like,' she said. 'It will be exactly like the smart parties you've taken me to in London. You'll all talk about films and places I've never seen and people I've never met. And everyone in the room will be at least twenty years older than I am. Can't you see that it will bore me stiff? I came out here to have a holiday – to enjoy myself.'

Graham listened to her wearily. He had met Martin Ford by chance outside the Minza Hotel that morning and had accepted the invitation because he thought it would amuse her.

'Fair enough,' he said. He crossed to the window which

101

overlooked a small patch of garden in the centre of a round-about. The dry heat of the evening was pleasant against his face. In the garden he could see a group of children playing in a circle. They were dancing round a small boy who pivoted on his heels in the centre of the ring, and as they danced he could hear their shrill young voices singing a Franco-Arab folk-song called 'Moustapha' which had become very popular after the war:

> 'Chérie, je t'aime,
> Chérie, je t'adore,
> Come la salsa
> Del pomodore.
> Ya Moustapha, ya Moustapha. . . .
> Quand je t'ai vue
> Sur le balcon,
> Tu m'as offert
> Une bonne cigarette
> Et tu m'as fait
> Perdre la tête.
> Chérie, je t'aime,
> Chérie, je t'adore. . . .'

The chanting stopped, and amidst giggles the child chose his true love. Together the couple moved to the edge of the circle and a blushing girl in pigtails was pushed into the middle, and the dance began again.

'Fair enough,' he repeated. 'If you don't want to come, then don't let's worry.'

3

HE stood looking out over the irregular roofs of the Kasbah which descended in layers into the town itself. From the roof-garden of Martin Ford's house there was a clear view of the expanse of Mediterranean beach that stretched past Tangier and curved in the distance towards Cap Malabata. The tranquil sea reflected the lights of the water-front.

Cole was perched on an iron balustrade at the edge of the terrace with a glass in his hand. Below him was a drop of ten feet on to the flat roof of an Arab house in the centre of which was an open skylight.

'Surprising how much cooler it is up here,' he said. 'I'm glad I brought a sweater.'

Graham peered over the railing. 'You're going to need more than a sweater if you fall through that hatch into someone's bedroom.'

Cole glanced down. 'I wonder if I'd have a sense of detachment while I was falling. They say you do.'

'I doubt it. You'd probably scream your head off.'

'Then let's move.'

They wandered to the other side of the terrace which overlooked the crowded patio.

'I'm glad you persuaded Vicky to come,' Cole said. 'When I last saw her she was obviously enjoying herself. And Martin Ford can't keep his beady eyes away from her.'

The marble fountain in the centre of the patio was surrounded by people who were laughing and holding long sticks in their hands.

103

'Can they be fishing for poor little goldfish?' Cole asked. 'Or do my eyes deceive me?'

'They don't deceive you. But the goldfish are made of celluloid with metal inside, and the hooks at the end of the rods are magnetic.'

Cole began to sniff deeply as they climbed down the stone staircase that linked the terraced garden on the roof with the courtyard below.

'Can't you smell it?'

'Smell what?'

Cole picked a sprig of the creeper that covered the wall.

'The jasmine, you zombie.'

'And all the evening I've been thinking it was your after-shave lotion.'

'Your trouble is that you've no sense of romance.'

'That's just what some of the critics said about *The Strawberry Patch*.'

As they reached the bottom of the stairs Martin Ford came towards them. He wore a toga made of brown shantung silk. He was a tall, stoutly-built man of about sixty. Thin curls of grey hair were plastered carefully around his scalp. With his fleshy, beaked nose, smooth cheeks, and rosebud lips and pompous manner, he managed without the aid of his costume to look like a debauched Roman emperor. He might well have dropped in at the party for a dissolute interlude on his way to the Senate.

'Where have you been, Graham?' he asked. 'I have missed your presence, but I have had the pleasure of conversing with the charming young lady you brought.'

Martin Ford waved a plump hand graciously at a passing guest and smiled.

'Not only is she beautiful,' he said in his soft delicate voice, mouthing each word as if Graham were deaf, 'but she is kind. And that is a very rare combination. Look at her now.'

Graham followed his glance and saw Vicky sitting on a bench under a fig tree. Beside her sat a squat old lady with white hair who was talking agitatedly as if a time-limit had been set for her discourse and she was running behind schedule. While her words rushed out she gesticulated with her glass, occasionally slopping drink over her shapeless bosom. And Vicky was listening to her intently, as if each phrase was important to her.

'When Isobel has a few drinks, there's no one in the entire community can abide her,' Martin Ford proclaimed. 'And that enchanting girl has stuck it out for ten whole minutes. She's a saint. But I suppose we ought to go and rescue her from martyrdom.'

He took Graham's arm and led him across the courtyard.

'Isobel,' he said, 'I want to introduce a distinguished friend of mine.'

'Go away,' the old lady said. 'Can't you see I'm busy?'

Vicky looked up at Graham and winked furtively.

'This is Graham Hadley,' Ford said firmly. 'He's come out to Morocco to make a film.'

'Then he can go home again,' the old lady said, tilting her glass so that gin spilled on to her lap. 'I don't like films, and I don't like film people.'

Ford's smile never faltered.

'Hadley's the exception,' he said.

'He doesn't look it,' the old lady said.

'Now you mustn't be prejudiced,' Martin Ford said suavely. 'An admission of prejudice, my dear Isobel, is an admission that one has stopped thinking.'

The old lady finished her drink and took another glass from the tray on the table beside her.

105

'Piss-elegant sod,' she said.

Ford straightened his toga.

'Now, Isobel,' he said, 'that's not the kind of language you use when addressing your Ladies' Guild.'

'Bugger my Ladies' Guild.'

Ford winced and turned his attention to Vicky and Graham. Spreading out the fingers of his right hand he extended his arm.

'I can see that you have both been admiring my ring,' he said, ignoring the old lady who had begun to hiccup into her handkerchief.

Vicky and Graham stared politely at the thick gold band on his index finger.

'I should tell you that I was fortunate in obtaining it through the good services of a friend of mine who shall remain nameless,' Ford said. 'It's quite a rare museum piece.'

'Like you,' the old lady said with an obscene cackle.

'Quite rare,' Ford continued steadily. 'It was found when they excavated Pompeii.'

'I think it's beautiful,' Vicky said.

'Not as beautiful as yourself,' Ford said with a courtly Roman bow. 'But I fear that I must rejoin my other guests.'

'And we must be off,' Graham said. 'Do you know, Vicky love, it's after twelve.'

'Heavens!' For a moment he was afraid she was going to refer to her appointment with Hamido. 'Thanks enormously for the party,' she said to her host. 'I really have enjoyed myself.'

'You shall come again – both of you,' Ford said as if conferring an imperial favour.

．　　　．　　　．　　　．　　　．

When they stopped the car in the narrow dimly-lit street they saw that the Coconut Bar was shut.

'Well, that's it,' Graham said. 'Would you like to try some other place? What about the Horseshoe Bar?'

'No. Let's get on home,' Vicky said.

The Boulevard de Paris was deserted except for a boy in jeans and a white shirt whom they did not know but who waved at the car.

'What time are we leaving for Tetuan?' Cole asked.

'Ten o'clock?' Graham suggested.

'More plans?' Vicky asked.

'Cole and I have to go and see the Governor of Tetuan to get permission to use locations in his district,' Graham said patiently. 'We told you three days ago, and you said you'd like to come with us for the ride. Remember?'

'Fine,' she said. 'At last I'll see something of the country-side.'

As Graham undressed he noticed that every chair in their bedroom was littered with Vicky's clothes. She had still not finished unpacking, and the clothes she had worn on the beach mingled with linen she had taken out of her suit-case that afternoon.

'You really are the most untidy girl I've ever known,' he said, trying not to sound like a schoolmaster. He picked up a piece of pink tissue-paper lying on the bed-cover. 'Has this any particular significance?'

Vicky was sitting at the dressing-table bathing her eyes.

'Yes,' she said. 'I've wrapped a pair of contact lenses in it. I've lost the case they were in.'

'Couldn't you put the paper in some container?'

'I will – in due course.'

Lying on top of one of her open suitcases he saw a small silver cigarette-case. He picked it up and saw that it had a late Victorian hallmark.

'Isn't it rather thin for cigarettes?' he asked.

Vicky turned round. The instant she saw what he was holding she moved quickly towards him and took it from his hand.

'It's a case for photographs,' she said, tucking it away at the bottom of a suitcase.

'Have I discovered where you hide the photos of all your boy-friends?'

'No.'

'Then why did you snatch it away from me?'

'I just don't like people to go rooting through my things.'

'I was trying to find a container for your lenses.'

Vicky took his hand.

'I know you were, Graham. I'm a little tired, so take no notice of me, and let's go to bed.'

The windows were open, and he had not pulled down the heavy shutter. He switched out the light, and they lay staring at the moon shining down on the flat roof-tops.

'I can smell it,' Vicky said in a drowsy voice. 'Can you? It's the smell that seems to pervade everything in the place, and perhaps all Morocco. . . . It's odd. . . . It's a sickly smell, and one feels it's centuries old. . . . It clings to all of them – even the young ones like Hamido. . . . It's a smell of sin. . . . But there's a smell of the earth, and the manger too.'

Vicky was soon asleep. But it was not until dawn had disturbed the privacy of his thoughts that Graham fell into a light doze.

4

THE flat now emanated a saline odour that came from a fusion of the butane gas in the kitchen with the smell of the disinfectant that the Fatima poured down the broken lavatory. Cole had been to see the obsequious French landlady who lived with a large Moroccan in the flat below, and she had promised to have a new bowl installed that very day. But so far nothing had been done. Tangier had a time-span all its own, Graham reflected as he put on the coat of the linen suit he was wearing in the Governor's honour, and left the bathroom.

Vicky was awake when he came into their bedroom.

'How are you this morning?' He adjusted the shutters and the sun cast a pattern on the bed like an aerial photograph of military trenches.

'I'm not feeling too well. It may be the inoculation. Or perhaps I had too much sun yesterday.'

He put his palm on her brow. 'You don't seem to be feverish.'

'I'm not sure one can tell like that. And I do feel ghastly. Do you think we should take my temperature? There's a thermometer in that black bag over there.'

He found the metal case stuck to a tube of face-cream. When he took the thermometer from her mouth, the reading was normal.

'A hundred and four,' he said. 'I think we should call a doctor.'

'A hundred and four?' She sat upright in bed. Then she saw his smile. 'What an idiot you can be. . . . But I think

I'll stay in bed all the same.' She turned on her side, away from the sun. He tried to hide his disappointment. 'A drive would do you good.'

'I feel I ought to stay here and relax.'

There was a knock at the door.

'Are you visible ?' Cole's voice asked.

'Completely.'

'The Governor has sent a car for us,' Cole said as he came in. 'The driver's just been up to the flat in a very smart uniform and half an hour early. If you look out of the window you can see the car – it's that vast grey Cadillac.'

'You're sure you won't come ?' Graham tried to make his voice sound indifferent because Cole was there.

Vicky pulled the sheets around her. 'Absolutely sure.'

'Vicky's not feeling too good,' Graham felt obliged to explain.

'Poor Vicky.'

Graham straightened his coat in the wardrobe mirror. The glass was not true, and it made him look one-eyed.

'We'll be back about dinner-time,' he said.

5

THE pavement outside the flat was still warm from the afternoon sun. The session in Tetuan with the Governor had been brief but successful, and they had returned sooner than they had expected. In the garden children were now playing a different game, but this time they were not singing. As Graham and Cole climbed up the third flight of stairs they could hear voices from inside the flat.

'Sounds as if Miss Tollard's entertaining,' Cole said as he unlatched the door.

In the living-room, Vicky was sitting on one of the black-leather chairs, bright-eyed and alert, talking to Hamido, who was sprawling on the sofa. She was dressed in white, and it contrasted with the colour of her skin which was now lightly tanned. The boy stood up as they came in. Graham looked at him without speaking.

'Was the meeting successful?' Vicky asked politely.

Graham was silent.

'Fine,' Cole said.

'At about noon I felt so much better that I decided to drive in the Chevrolet to the Atlantic beach. And I met Hamido on the way, so he came with me.' Vicky's explanation was delivered so smoothly that she had evidently taken trouble to prepare it – unless it was the truth.

Hamido was standing by the sofa. Graham was savagely glad that he had not sat down again.

'I didn't even know you had a driving licence,' Graham said.

Vicky brushed away a fly that had settled on her beach

111

trousers. 'The keys were on the hall table, and I drive rather well. I hope you don't mind me taking the car?'

His hands were sweating. The suit he had put on for the Governor suddenly seemed tight. Without looking round he knew that Cole was watching him.

'Not at all,' he said and walked out into the hall.

'Where are you off to?' Vicky called out.

'I'm just off to change.'

Graham walked along the corridor and pushed open the door of their bedroom. The shutter was down and he strode across and tugged at the canvas band on the side of the window to pull it up. The room was a jumble of untidiness. Vicky's clothes had spilled over from the chairs on to the carpet, and her shoes were strewn like shells across the floor. The bed had been made and the green silk cover was unrumpled, but he felt that in some way the room would confirm what he suspected. He drew back the cover and ran his fingers along the pillow. Then he smelled his hand. His eyes searched round the room and fixed on the ashtray. There were several stubs in it. He picked up one of them and smoothed out the wrinkled paper on the cigarette. It was a cheap Moroccan brand that cost a dirham a packet. As he wrenched off his tie he heard the silk tear.

Vicky was alone when he returned to the living-room.

'Where's Cole?' he asked.

'He offered to drive Hamido home.' Her face was set in defiant lines of obstinacy.

'How appropriate that you're wearing white,' he said.

'Sorry?'

'Your clothes – white shirt, white slacks, white sandals. It's all so virginal.'

'I see.'

His fingers found the gold ring and began twisting it.

'Aren't you going to say anything?'

112

She sighed. 'What can I say?'

'I'm waiting.'

'But I've told you already. I told you that I only liked boys of my own age. I warned you this would happen. Be honest – didn't I? But I also promised that you'd have first call. And you have.'

'It was deceit.'

'Only because I didn't want to hurt you.'

'You took him to our room.'

'I didn't want to. But we couldn't go back to his place.'

'So you took him to our bed.'

When she stood up he noticed that she was wearing her blue contact lenses. They gave her a spurious look of innocence. Her hands were quivering as she spoke.

'It's a bed, isn't it? Not an altar. It's not sacred. Why do you have to dramatize the whole thing? I haven't betrayed you in any way. Let's face it – you knew exactly what you were getting when you started all this.'

'And you can't see what I feel?'

'Evidently not.'

'You can't see what it'll be like for me – now that I know you've been with him?'

'What's wrong with him? He's perfectly clean. In fact, I've never known a smoother skin.'

'That wasn't what I meant. But even so – how can you possibly tell? He may be diseased for all you know.'

'So might you.'

Suddenly Vicky laughed, and Graham crossed over as she stood beside the empty fireplace and rested his hands on her shoulders. But her arms remained at her side with fingers clenched.

'I don't want to hurt you,' she said. 'If you feel you've made a mistake, please don't feel under any obligation towards me.' She raised her head so that her eyes were almost

113

level with his. 'Would you rather I left and went to live in some hotel?'

There was no guile in her voice. This was neither a petulant proposal that could be casually withdrawn nor a smart manœuvre to gain ground. The question was direct and seriously intended, and it was one that left him without defence or argument.

'You know I wouldn't,' he said.

He could feel her pulse beating through the thin cotton shirt.

'Vicky,' he said. 'I'm trying to be reasonable. Won't you meet me half-way?'

She removed his hands from her shoulders, held them for a moment and then turned away to the highly-coloured tapestry that hung on the wall.

'You're being very reasonable, I know,' she said. 'But it's not a question of meeting you half-way. You see, when I face up to our relationship I realize that part of me resents you. I can't exactly say why. Perhaps it's because it puts me in a difficult position. And why does it? Because if it's to last at all, then either I've got to give up my liberty or I've got to be dishonest with you.'

The tapestry portrayed a blue-clad huntsman on a white horse hurling a spear at a yellow gazelle. With her forefinger outstretched Vicky began tracing the crude pattern of the sunset in the background.

'You've agreed to my terms – which you can't keep,' she said. 'If I agreed to your terms I'd be cheating you. And there it is. I told you from the start it wouldn't work. And it can't. If I didn't care for you at all, I'd string along for the good time. But I *am* fond of you, and I can't bear to make you unhappy.'

Vicky was now stroking the head of the stricken yellow deer.

114

'There *is* no half-way mark,' she said. 'Either I'm faithful to you or I'm not. . . . You're patient and sweet, and you hope I'll change. But I can't help how I'm made. Believe me, I hate it when I'm bitchy to you and I can see that I'm making you sad. I can't go on taking everything from you and giving nothing in return. It's got to end. Mind you, if there was a chance that I could become what you want, it would be worth it. But there isn't, Graham. And one of us has to make the break.'

She had turned back to him, and her brow was puckered in a frown. For a moment he forced himself to face the prospect of Vicky's leaving him that evening. In his mind, he could see her picking up the strewn clothes from the carpet and pushing them into a suitcase. He heard her telephone for a taxi. He watched her carrying her bags down the flight of echoing stairs. He saw her forlorn yet arrogant expression as she got into the *chico-taxi*. He heard the metallic ring as the door slammed. He stood in the dark porch, watching the little car drive up the empty street, and he waited until its lights had mingled in the flickering stream of illumination in the main road beyond. Then he turned back into the hall.

Graham shuddered.

'It's a bed,' Vicky had said, 'not an altar.' And perhaps that explained why he could not accept her infidelity. From his past, drifting from the chancel steps of a misty church in Birmingham, came the words used in the ceremony – 'with my body I thee worship'. And God – if there were a God – knew that with his body he worshipped Vicky. Their bed had become his altar, and to him it was sacred. And in a way, he thought, it was Graham Hadley who was the sacrifice. What had Cole said? 'You'll lose your peace of mind, and if you lose that you lose everything.' Perhaps that was what he was sacrificing, he thought. But he would

have no peace of mind if she left him, and he might yet find
some if she stayed.

'No,' he said to Vicky. 'I couldn't bear it. I'd rather have
a little of you than none. So let's play it by ear – both of us.
And let's try to make it work.'

6

EVELYN ROPER strode towards the Chevrolet in her heavy brown-leather shoes, walking with her feet splayed out like a Moroccan wearing *babouches*. An old woman who squatted on the pavement outside the Minza Hotel selling matches shifted her position to allow Evelyn to pass and stared oddly after her.

Evelyn flung open the car door nearest to Vicky and sat down.

'I've passed that old woman every day for the last two years,' she said, 'and she still looks at me as if I were a freak. However, I suppose I shouldn't let it bother me.'

They drove down the hill into the Zoco Grande and left the car by the fruit stalls that were clustered in one corner of the crowded market-square. A small boy in a torn denim shirt clutched Graham's arm. 'Des oranges? Des raisins, M'sieur?' he asked in a beseeching whine.

'Va t'en,' Evelyn said sharply. 'Sirf 'hallek.' The boy craned his neck to glance up at her and scuttled away.

'You have to be firm in these parts,' Evelyn explained as she led them under an archway into the Rue des Siaghines. Moroccans in black or brown djellabas, hordes of children, veiled women teetering on stiletto heels, Berbers in white woollen robes were swarming along the narrow cobbled street, and from the shops that lined each side merchants called out to them. In a tailor's shop, a spindly, anaemic-looking man with rimless spectacles was being measured for a suit, and behind him they could hear the sound of

117

sewing-machines that continued incessantly like a plant generating electricity.

Evelyn jostled her way through the crowd, now and then stepping aside reluctantly to let a donkey laden with bulging sacks or thick bundles of brushwood pass. Flies swarmed round piles of dung, and the lane seemed impregnated with the acrid smell of bodies and of incense and of fruit slowly drying in the sun. A young girl in a torn bodice approached Vicky, cradling a child in her arms. Matted dusty hair fell around her face, and her large eyes were uplifted as she extended a claw-like hand. Vicky stopped.

'Come along!' Evelyn said impatiently. 'They're taught to beg before they can even walk. If you'd been born here, you'd probably be at it yourself.'

Vicky searched in her bag and gave the girl a coin. 'That's just what I was thinking,' she replied.

They turned right into a dark passage and Evelyn stopped.

'If you look up there you'll see the street-sign in Arabic,' she said. 'It's called the Alley of Goldsmiths.'

Evelyn acknowledged the servile bow of a shopkeeper who had recognized her with a curt inclination of her head. Graham could see her as the austere Lady Evelyn in an early silent film, stepping across the drawbridge through lines of cringing serfs.

The only light that reached the small dingy shop they now entered came from the passage outside. Two hard-backed chairs faced a counter made of unvarnished planks of wood behind which crouched an old macerated figure with a wispy beard and features sharpened by illness. The old man rose stiffly to his feet and greeted Evelyn warily. She leaned imperiously on the counter and the boards creaked under her weight.

'We want to see some bracelets,' she declared.

The man nodded his head, unlocked the squat safe in the corner behind him, drew out a tray, and placed it on the counter. The bracelets were of heavy gold, finely worked in traditional Moorish designs. The choice finally lay between three of them.

'How much is this one?' Evelyn managed to hold the bracelet like a tankard of beer. The old man took it and weighed it delicately on the scales.

'We only charge for the price of gold,' he said. 'We do not charge for the workmanship.'

'I know that,' said Evelyn. 'How much?'

'This one? Five hundred dirham.'

Evelyn swayed back from the counter and gave a horse-laugh. 'Five hundred dirhams for a bangle! What about the other?'

The jeweller reached out for the bracelet. 'This? Four hundred and fifty dirham.'

Evelyn paid no further attention to him and turned to Vicky.

'How many are you buying?'

'Two,' Graham replied.

'It's certainly the devil of a choice.' She began to clasp a bracelet on Vicky's arm.

'So I was right!' The voice which came unexpectedly from behind Graham was loud and petulant. 'I was told I'd find you here.'

In the doorway stood a short chubby girl of about twenty-five wearing a pair of winged sun-glasses rimmed with powdered crystal. Her bleached hair hung loosely over her forehead which was already marked with lines of peevishness.

Evelyn's hand dropped from Vicky's wrist, leaving the bracelet unfastened.

'Susan!' she barked. 'What are you doing here?'

The girl stalked in, her face radiant in anticipation of a row.

'What indeed!' She looked Vicky up and down. 'So this is her.'

Graham glanced at Vicky. She was standing erect and detached like an onlooker. Evelyn advanced towards Susan.

'Look here, you blonde bombshell,' she began firmly. 'I don't want a peep out of *you*. And take off those ridiculous glasses when I'm talking to you. . . .'

'I certainly won't.' The girl caught sight of the bracelet on Vicky's arm and snorted like a colt.

'This,' she said, pointing to Vicky's wrist, 'is the final betrayal. The end.'

'She was all of two years at the Bognor rep,' Evelyn explained in a strident aside.

The girl took off her sun-glasses as she noticed Graham. 'And who is *he*?' she asked, glowering at him. 'Her father?'

'No,' Evelyn replied. 'The vicar. Haven't you met?'

The girl's attention switched back to Vicky. Her self-assurance was dwindling.

'Anyway,' Evelyn continued briskly, 'will you please excuse us.' She picked up another bracelet and began to fasten it on Vicky's arm.

The girl brushed aside a strand of bleached hair and waved her finger menacingly. 'Don't think I'm going to take this lying down, Evelyn Roper.'

'But how else?'

Tears of frustration streaked the girl's cheeks. 'I never thought it would come to this,' she said, putting on her sun-glasses. 'Never.' And suddenly she was gone.

Evelyn once again seemed absorbed in choosing the bracelets. She looked up and saw Graham watching her.

'Don't worry. This could only happen in Tangier,' she

said cheerfully. 'I think those two are the prettiest, don't you?'

Vicky was silent.

'Don't you?' Evelyn repeated.

'Yes, I do.'

Evelyn addressed the jeweller who had been gaping vacantly at the scene from behind the counter.

'Eight hundred and fifty dirhams for both.'

The old man opened his mouth to speak.

'Or we'll go next door. Take it or leave it.'

The wrinkled lips slid into a smile, but the weary eyes glinted with hatred.

'Very good,' the old man said. 'Eight fifty.'

Outside the light was harsh against their eyes. When they reached the Zoco Grande, Evelyn hailed a taxi.

'I have to rush,' she said. 'See you later.'

She was waving to them from across the dusty square by the time Graham realized he had forgotten to thank her.

'It's like being caught up by a whirlwind,' Vicky said. 'I think I need a drink.' She tapped his shoulder. 'And thanks very much,' she added.

They drove up the hill to the Minza. Vicky's arm was outstretched so that she could admire the intricate design of the heavy gold bands that she had put on her left wrist, so that they contrasted with the two thin bracelets he had noticed the first evening they met.

'I feel like a kept woman,' she said as they wandered into the bar. Cole was sitting with his back to the swimming-pool clenching a gin-fizz and examining the full-length oil portrait of the Caïd Maclean on the wall opposite. As he waved to them, his eyes fastened on Vicky's new bracelets.

'Why! Hullo, Bangles!' he said.

7

GRAHAM glanced out of the window of the flat, finished the whisky that Cole had poured out for him, and walked over to the drink-table to help himself to another. These last few days he knew he had been drinking heavily, but he could no more control his urge for the anaesthesia that liquor produced than he could curb his irritation.

'I'm not coming,' Vicky repeated, her face sullen with obstinacy. In answer came a grinding resolute voice that Graham was vaguely conscious was his own.

'From the moment we landed in Tangier,' the voice said, 'you've been nothing but a prize bitch. You must learn to give *something*.'

He noticed Vicky's face, contorted with exasperation.

'You don't understand a thing,' she said. 'You don't see how claustrophobic Tangier can be. The four walls are so terribly close. I've got to get away from you both for a while or I'll suffocate. Can't you realize that I have to have some time to myself?'

'You're not doing so badly. You've spent the last two days on the beach – in your element with Hamido fawning over you.'

Cole looked up from the book he was pretending to read and leaned forward.

'How's your drink, Bangles?' he asked.

'Fine, thanks.'

Graham made an effort to restrain his temper.

'I'm not coming to another grand party, so let's leave it at that,' Vicky said. 'But it's nothing to do with you. That's

what you won't appreciate. I just want to be on my own –
if only for an hour or two.'

'Be on your own!' Graham exclaimed.

Cole gave a start and adjusted his reading-glasses.
'Please,' he said. 'The acoustics aren't that bad.'

'I'd accept all this jazz about claustrophobia and getting
away from us, but for one fact.' Graham's voice was sub-
dued but crisp. 'And that fact is that "being on your own"
means a jaunt round the sordid little bars of Tangier with
an equally sordid little garage mechanic.'

'Anything you say. But I'm not going to the party.'

The electric geyser rumbled monotonously overhead.
Graham stood up. 'Then we'll leave you to be alone. But I
suggest you take off all your jewellery before you meet
him, and I advise you to take just enough money with you
to pay for the drinks.'

At the crossing Graham looked to the left for oncoming
cars.

'Isn't that Vicky waiting on the corner?' Cole said.

Her head was turned away from them.

'You're right. It is.' Graham slowed down.

'Don't stop,' Cole said.

Graham hesitated. 'Why not?'

'You must let her have some freedom. That's your only
hope.'

'Maybe.'

'Not maybe. Definitely.'

In silence Graham drove up the hill towards the Marshan
and turned right to the Kasbah. He knew his way to the
villa, for it belonged to a successful dress-designer with
whom he had stayed on his last visit to Tangier. The Place

de la Kasbah was filled with rows of cars, and the young Moroccan policeman directed them into a convenient space. As the car drew up, gangs of urchins rushed forward and pressed their faces against the windows. A watchman was standing by a small wooden hut at the entrance to the villa, and at their approach he pulled open the heavy brass-studded door which had been left in place when the old building was modernized. A Moroccan servant in an embroidered silver waistcoat above drooping pantaloons led them through a vast hall towards the clatter of voices that came from the central patio.

The guests were standing in clusters beneath the white Moorish arches that flanked a rectangular swimming-pool, tiled in mosaic. Flambeaux in copper urns blazed at each corner of the pool, and smoke was drifting through the open roof into the cloudless sky.

Cole took his arm. 'Do you know Nancy Drew?' he whispered.

Graham shook his head. 'No. Should I?'

'No reason. She's standing by the pillar on your right. It's a sad story. She nearly made the grade in the thirties in Hollywood. Then she lost her husband in the war and retired, and a few years ago she got six months for passing dud cheques. I think I'll go and have a word with her.'

Cole threw out his arms as he approached the woman and embraced her several times. Graham moved away and stood gazing down into the pool. In the light of the flickering torch the water reflected his figure which might have belonged to a young man. Graham sighed.

'Be careful I don't push you in.' He recognized the cackle. It was the old lady from Martin Ford's party.

'You'll have forgotten my name, and I've certainly forgotten yours. I'm Isobel King.'

'Graham Hadley,' he replied.

She hovered precariously at the edge of the pool. 'I liked that young beauty you brought to Martin's party,' she announced. 'She's a good girl, that one. Anyone who's prepared to listen to me when I've had a few noggins gets full marks.'

Graham smiled at her, and she nodded her head several times in assent to some unspoken remark. She was swaying a little. Suddenly she threw out her arm and pointed at him with a quivering finger.

'I have a word of advice for you,' she declared in a deep oracular voice. 'A word of advice.' She looked away from him and saw a waiter approaching with a tray of drinks. With a carefree gesture she tossed her empty glass into the pool and seized a drink from the tray.

'What was I saying?' she asked.

'You had a word of advice for me.'

'That's right. So I had. But now I simply can't remember what it was. You don't have a cigar by any chance?'

'I'm afraid not.'

'Can't be helped. I'll have to do without . . . I was giving you a word of advice. That's correct. And now I recollect what it was.'

The old lady took a sip of her drink and grimaced.

'Vodka,' she said. 'And I wanted gin.' Again the glass splashed into the pool. She wiped her lips with a large foulard handkerchief. 'I'm the seventh child of a seventh child so you pay heed to me,' she said. 'Just be there when she really needs you, and you'll find that in time you'll get what you want.' She inhaled deeply and then sighed as if her utterance had exhausted her. 'And now,' she said, 'would you be so kind as to get me a large gin?'

'With tonic?' Graham asked.

'With nothing,' she replied.

Graham found a bottle of gin on a sideboard and poured

out half a glass, but when he returned to the pool the old lady had gone. He glanced down at the pool but the water was clear and tranquil. He smiled to himself as the words she had spoken so portentously churned in his mind. 'When she really needs you.' He was amused by his eagerness to accept advice that he wanted to hear. And now, with an idiotic romanticism that he could not repress, he wished that Vicky were there to share the charm of the patio so that she could look up at the sky and see the same stars that he saw. Perhaps she was still waiting on the corner of that empty street. Or perhaps the street was no longer empty. 'They can get quite nasty when there's a gang of them together,' Evelyn had said. Possibly the old woman – seventh child of a seventh child – was gifted with second sight.

He found Cole and tapped him on the shoulder.

'I'm going now. Would you mind taking a taxi back?'

'Not at all.'

'And could you say good-bye to our host? I haven't seen him all evening.'

'Nor will you,' said Cole. 'He was flying from Paris this morning, but the plane's been delayed.'

'So who's been giving the party?'

Cole chuckled. 'I've been wondering myself. But that's Tangier for you.'

Graham beamed at Nancy Drew and left. A young boy guided out the car with precise hand-signals, and Graham gave him a dirham.

When he reached the corner, at first he thought Vicky had gone. But she was standing on the opposite side of the street. He turned the heavy wheel and slowly let out the clutch. The car stopped close to her. He leaned across to open the door, and without a word she got in and sat down beside him.

. . . . .

126

Vicky sat on the edge of the bed staring dully at a gazelle-skin rug.

Graham's voice was gentle. 'I know Moroccans. I know Hamido's type. And if you're trying to make him fall in love with you, then you're going about it the wrong way.'

She was silent but he had not expected a reply.

'You haven't spent any money on yourself, so I suppose that I'm paying for his keep as well as yours. Has he bought anything for you – with the money you've given him?' At once he regretted the remark. The draught from the corridor pushed open the door and he stood up to close it. When he turned round she was arranging the bottles and jars of cosmetics that littered the dressing-table.

'Think of it,' he said. 'You were kept waiting for over an hour on a street-corner. . . . Where's your pride gone to?'

He could see the smooth skin at the nape of her neck as her head drooped forward in dejection. Her words were muffled. 'What do you suggest I do?' she asked.

He had expected to feel some pleasure at winning his point, but her defeat brought him no triumph. His limbs were leaden with fatigue.

'Try, just a little, to love me,' he said. 'Because you know that with me you won't be hurt.'

Vicky's head turned slightly towards him, and her hands carved the air in a despondent gesture like a chess-player who knows that the previous move has made a checkmate inevitable.

'Look,' she said, 'I'll never see him again. Will that make you happy?'

8

THE roof of the disused customs shed at the former Spanish-Moroccan frontier had fallen in, and weeds grew where the soil from the window-boxes had tumbled on to the concrete. The road narrowed at a bridge that spanned a dried-up watercourse, and Vicky slowed down. At first Graham had been nervous of her driving but he had soon realized that she handled the car well.

The last two days had been disturbing. On the morning after Vicky had made her promise to give up Hamido, Cole had left early for the mountain village of Chauen to explore locations. An hour later Graham had set out with Vicky for the Atlantic beach. He could remember each detail of the scene as vividly as if he had directed it. . . .

He carried Vicky's beach-bag down the resounding stairs, and Vicky put on her sun-glasses as they walked through the hall towards the glare of the street outside. The Chevrolet was parked in the shade of the block of flats opposite, and close beside it on the corner by the garden a young man in jeans and a blue singlet was waiting. It was Hamido, and as they crossed the road he gazed at Vicky with a fierce eagerness.

'Pretend you haven't seen him,' Vicky said.

But the boy was now standing no more than a few yards away from her. He took a step towards her, and Vicky looked straight ahead as if there was no one in sight.

128

Hamido stopped. He must have understood that she intended to ignore him, for he made no attempt to speak to her. Vicky passed by him and walked quickly towards the Chevrolet. As the car moved off the boy gave her a sad, hesitant wave of his hand.

Vicky was quiet throughout the day on the beach beyond the Caves of Hercules, dozing in the sun. They lunched late in the afternoon at a small restaurant run by a Frenchman and his wife and watched Chleu boys wearing the belts of Berber women dancing on the terrace. Vicky spoke little, and Graham hoped that in her silent meditation she appreciated that he had not been wholly selfish.

When they returned to Tangier in the evening, Hamido was leaning against the low wall of the house opposite, smoking a cigarette. As the car drew up he threw down the cigarette and ground it into the pavement with his heel.

'Don't look,' Vicky said.

But when Graham unlatched the main door leading into the hall and held it open for her, he knew that Vicky must have glanced back, for he saw the boy's hand fall quickly to his side in the termination of some furtive gesture.

The Fatima had cooked a chicken for dinner. Graham had decided not to attempt to change Vicky's mood, and they ate in silence. Overhead the geyser rumbled and gurgled in the quiet of the night and plates rattled in the kitchen.

An hour after midnight Graham awoke. Vicky was curled up like a child beside him with her fingers touching her lips. He slid quietly from the bed and crossed to the window and peered out. By the light of the street-lamp he could see the boy clearly. He was crouched on the wall of the house opposite, his elbows on his knees, his face cradled in his hands, staring straight up at their window, and for a while it seemed to Graham that their eyes met and locked in a silent struggle. Later he wondered if this recognition had been imagined, for he had stared back unwaveringly, and suddenly the boy had slithered down from the wall, stretched his arms and strolled away.

Early the following morning when they crossed the street, the wall was deserted. But as they approached the car, Hamido appeared from round the corner and walked towards them. A tacit agreement had now arisen between them not to mention the boy's vigil. Graham put the suit-cases into the boot of the Chevrolet and closed it.

'Can I drive?' Vicky asked.

When the car passed him, Hamido looked fixedly at Vicky. Suddenly his lips twisted and he put his hand to his mouth as if to bite it. Then Graham understood that by taking the wheel Vicky was showing the boy that she herself had made the decision to leave. . . .

Slowly the car climbed into hilly desolate country until, to the south-east, they could see the long uneven range of the Rif mountains stretched across the horizon. Towards noon they turned a steep bend in the cork-screw road and looked across the valley at the village of Chauen sprawling between the horns of two mountains. A narrow lane running between whitewashed houses with blue-painted window-sills and brown-tiled Andalusian roofs led to the hotel.

'The boys will take your things,' Cole said impatiently. 'Come and look at the view.'

He led them through the hotel, past the restaurant and the reception desk, and drew them on to a broad, red-tiled terrace with a swimming-pool at the far end.

130

'Now,' he said, stretching his arms wide with pride as if he had created the panorama.

To the right they could see light-green fields and dark-green olive groves tumbling down the slope to the river that trickled through the valley along its stony bed, dried by the heat of summer, and the road curling like a dark-blue snake down the flank of the tawny mountain. Across the valley, perched on top of the hill, was a small white-washed mosque, its trim crenellated outline sharp against the sky. Half-way up the mountainside like butterflies on a brown cloth six or seven white-hooded women, their robes billowing in a light breeze, wandered down the winding path that dipped into the valley and led to the cluster of bright houses to their left.

Vicky had moved to the pool.

'I'm going to change for a swim,' she said. 'Coming?' The stiff lines had been smoothed from her face, and her voice rang with happiness.

The two beds in their oblong room were placed sideways against one wall and along it ran a light-coloured wooden beam with bolts protruding at intervals of two feet. As they undressed Vicky began to unscrew one of them.

'I'm sure these bolts are terribly symbolic,' she said. 'But I simply can't imagine what purpose they serve.'

She crossed to the window and looked across the valley.

'I'm glad we came here,' she said.

Later, as he watched her diving into the pool, Cole turned to Graham. 'I think it's going to be all right,' he murmured.

9

Vicky had been pleased to discover that they could have breakfast on the terrace by the swimming-pool. From across the little table Graham watched her with a contentment almost amounting to complacency. Vicky put down the croissant she had dipped into her coffee and waved away some flies that were settling on the strawberry jam.

'We need a fly-swatter,' she said. 'My father has one he bought in India, and he's the best fly-swatter I know.'

'Shall I meet your parents one of these days?'

Vicky frowned. 'It wouldn't do at all. They'd be highly suspicious. You have the kind of ardent look about you that would put them on their guard as soon as they clapped eyes on you. And incidentally, what are you looking so pleased about this morning?'

'Because I've found out something.'

'Such as?'

'Part of you may resent me, but part of you quite needs me.'

'What makes you think so?'

Graham put down his cup.

'In one's sleep,' he said, 'one can do things that are very revealing.'

'Meaning what?'

'In your sleep last night you suddenly put your arms round me and clung to me frantically as if you were afraid I'd escape from you. You simply wouldn't let me go.'

Vicky smiled. 'That may not prove anything,' she said.

'You see, I expect I was thinking about my poor dear panda.'

'Panda?'

'When I was a child I had a black-and-white toy panda, and I loved him very much. And one day I gave him a bath and put him on the stone ledge of the fireplace to dry – dangerously close to the log fire. When my Ma came into the nursery she saw him propped up there and she said, "Panda's going to fall in." And I said, "No, he's not." But he did. He toppled over right into the fire.'

Vicky crumpled the napkin with her hands.

'I tried to pull him out, and I'm certain I could have pulled him out. But my Ma dragged me back because she was afraid I'd get burnt. "He'll have to go," she said. And I had to watch him burning. And all the time I was sure I could have saved him.'

Vicky spread out the napkin and began to fold it neatly.

'I don't think I ever got over panda's cremation,' she said.

'Did they never buy you another one?'

Her eyes had turned towards two children splashing in the pool.

'No,' she said. 'They didn't.'

Suddenly she seemed to have lost interest in the conversation.

She stretched out her hand. 'Can you give me a cigarette?' she asked.

10

GRAHAM noticed that they were the only people left in the restaurant. They moved out with their drinks on to the terrace so that the waiters could go to bed. Vicky put down her glass and the bracelets tinkled on her wrist. 'It's odd,' she said. 'But I can drink vodka all evening, and it hasn't the slightest effect.'

Graham looked at Cole and winked. Vicky sighed. 'Do you know what I feel like doing?'

'We haven't a clue,' Cole said.

Vicky waved her hand towards the dark outline of the mountains.

'I feel like taking an Alfa-Romeo whizzing over the hills and far away.'

Graham picked up his gold case from the table and stood up. 'Well, I think you ought to be a little less ambitious and whizz off to bed,' he said. 'Come along.' Vicky sighed and rose from her chair.

'Good night, children,' Cole called after them.

'I really must write a book,' Vicky said as they climbed up the stairs to their bedroom. 'But I can't think of anything to write about.'

'That would present a problem,' Graham agreed.

They had left their room unlocked, the Berber maid had tidied away Vicky's clothes, and the sheets of the beds were turned down. Vicky went to the open window and leaned out, grasping the handle that wound up the shutter to balance herself.

'The mosque looks wonderful at night,' she said. 'It seems to be luminous.'

He put his arm round her and together they looked out across the valley. The headlight of a motor-cycle darted along the mountainside like a firefly and then disappeared at a bend in the road. Vicky's head was touching his shoulder, and at that instant he was aware of a concord between them so much more complete than at any other stage of their friendship that he felt he could afford to ask the question that haunted him.

'Do you miss him?'

Vicky slipped her hand into his pocket, took out his case, and lit a cigarette with her lighter.

'I do in some ways. And so I suppose the answer must be "yes",' she said softly. 'There's an old folk-song called "Fare thee well, my honey". I adore the words "fare thee well", don't you? They mean so much more than "good-bye" . . . You know, Hamido was very sweet and very attractive. And it's so easy to fall for someone beautiful.'

She was now talking to him without inhibition, as if he were a priest in a confessional that she would never visit again.

'You see,' Vicky said, 'Hamido was very interesting in his way. He was an odd mixture of a self-assured adult and an uncertain child. Most of the time he told me lies, and I knew he was lying. For instance, one afternoon I went to tea with him at Porte's, and who should we run into but Martin Ford – I hardly recognized him in a suit. When I introduced Hamido, Martin stared at him hard. "I feel sure I met you some time ago in Tangier with a friend of mine," Martin said in that pompous voice of his. "Have you a brother who drives a taxi?" '

Graham felt a sudden annoyance that Martin Ford should have seen her with the boy.

'And then?' he asked.

'Well, Hamido said he'd never met Martin before in his life, and I happened to mention that Hamido was a mechanic. Then Martin did look surprised. "I never forget a face," he said to me. "I am convinced it is the same one." And he turned back to Hamido and glared at him. "You are a mechanic," he said accusingly. "And your brother has a taxi." Hamido looked very awkward and shook his head and said he hadn't even got a brother. But I knew this was a lie because he'd already told me that he had one.'

'Perhaps it was *you* he was lying to?' Graham suggested.

'That's very possible. I suppose if you're really poor you don't have much time for morals. Though I don't even know if he *is* poor. His father's dead and his mother lives in Fez. She's Berber, incidentally, and that's where his violet eyes come from. When he was a child they only just had enough money to eat. With any luck at the end of the week his mother would give Hamido and his little brother two dirhams to go to the cinema, and that was all the money they'd get.'

Graham moved his arm into a more comfortable position. 'He's certainly not living on two dirhams a week in Tangier,' he said. 'He dresses quite well for a young Moroccan.'

'I suppose he earns something from the garage. Have you noticed he's got quite an expensive lighter? I asked him how he came by it and he said he'd shown an American woman round Fez and she'd given it him as a present. And he certainly had some money that morning when we drove out to the Atlantic beach – the day you went to Tetuan – because he paid for drinks at the restaurant.'

Three house-martins swooped down and settled on the railing beyond the pool.

'You know, he was awfully sweet, and I do believe that in his way he was quite fond of me. But somehow he never

136

seemed to be at ease. It was almost as if there was someone following him and he had to keep looking over his
shoulder. He was always preoccupied. He worried. Something trivial would happen and he'd get nervous. For
instance, we were driving to the beach that day, when a
white car came towards us. Suddenly Hamido put up his
hand to shield his face and turned away. When he saw me
looking at him he slid his hand down his cheek as if he
were wiping off sweat. He said he felt boiling hot, but I'd
got all the windows open. He was obviously afraid of being
seen. There'd been nobody at the side of the road, so it
must have been someone in that white car that scared
him.'

Vicky took a deep breath and exhaled it slowly, almost
regretfully. 'But I was happy that day,' she said. 'It was all
rather fun. We went down on to the beach beyond the
Caves of Hercules. We were lying on that huge towel you
gave me, and it was really rather silly – but he kept leaning
across and kissing me. I suppose he *was* behaving badly
considering that anyone could have seen us.'

When Vicky paused Graham knew that she was leaving
out details for his benefit. But he could see the boy's stubby
fingers sliding down from her shoulders leaving a trail of
sand on her oiled skin while his lips searched her mouth.

'Then what happened?'

Graham tried to control the betraying quiver of the
muscle in his arm.

'We drove along the beach to Cap Spartel and had a real
drama,' Vicky said. 'The wheels of the Chevrolet got embedded in the sand. People came and tried to help us push
it out, but the wheels just sank deeper. So I left Hamido
guarding the car and got a lift into town to find a break-
down lorry. I asked at three garages for a *camion-remor-
queur* without any success. But at the fourth garage the

137

F

proprietor came out. He was a stout Frenchman of about sixty with blubber lips and bushy eyebrows, and when I told him my problem he gave me a leer and said he'd come out himself in a Land-Rover. There was a minor battle each time he changed gear, but I managed to fight him off, and we arrived safely at Cap Spartel. And there was Hamido in his skin-tight cotton trousers and red T-shirt waiting by the Chevrolet.

'When Hamido saw the man with me, he went quite pale. He was obviously scared stiff. My stout companion gave a grunt. Then he put his hands on his hips and stood in front of Hamido with a nasty expression on his face, looking him up and down with contempt. "Tu n'as pas l'air tellement malade," he said. And then I realized the form. My lecherous companion was the owner of the garage where Hamido worked. Hamido had evidently sent a message to say that he'd been ill, and now he'd been caught out.

'"I can see precisely why you've been laid up all week," the garage-owner said, leering towards me. I was livid, but Hamido said nothing. He just stood there. It was rather pathetic to see him change from a proud escort to a brow-beaten garage-hand.'

In the garden below the hotel a dog was howling to the moon.

'After that night when he'd kept you waiting,' Graham said, 'why did he come back to the flat and lurk outside all day and night?'

'I'm not sure,' Vicky answered. 'Perhaps he wanted to explain why he hadn't turned up that evening. I don't know. But I'd promised you I'd never see him again, so it was a bit late, wasn't it? All the same, I suppose I should have given him a present. I'm sure all his other girl-friends have.'

Graham was saddened by the tinge of bitterness in her

138

voice. Perhaps he had been foolish to suppose that distance would help her forget. A cloud had covered the moon, and the dog had stopped howling.

'Whatever you'd given him wouldn't make much difference to his life,' Graham said. 'When you gave him a meal I expect you got the impression that he didn't need to eat. These people have a strange mentality. For example, all those boys smoke, but there's no craving, no need for cigarettes. They aren't grateful if you give them one, and if they haven't got a packet they go without.'

Vicky was staring down into the valley.

'It's odd,' she said. 'Hamido works in a garage and hates the filth of it. His only ambition is to run a beach-bar like Evelyn's. He's talked to me about that bar for hours on end. He even knows what colour he's going to paint it. Yet he'd never make any constructive move, however small, towards getting a beach-bar, though he told me it was his life's ambition.'

'Perhaps he hoped you'd put up some money and go in with him as a partner.'

'Perhaps.' Vicky moved away from the window and began playing with one of the ornamental bolts beside her bed. 'I don't know, and I don't care now,' she said. 'But he was very sweet, and he had his good points.'

Graham leaned against the window-ledge and watched her slowly undress.

11

An old woman shuffled on to the terrace, stooped down to attach a hose-pipe to a tap at the corner of the pool, and began to spray the red tiles. The sun was beginning to set, and the valley was already in darkness. Cole held out his finger and waved it like a wand.

'One week,' he said. 'And only one location. It's not good enough.'

'Then let's move farther up into the mountains where the scenery's more stark,' Graham suggested.

Cole smoothed back his hair.

'Right,' he said. 'When do we start?'

'Tomorrow morning?'

'Fine.'

'I'll book us rooms at Ketama.'

'What about the Pasha here?'

'We can see him on our way back.'

Graham watched Vicky as she came into the hotel through the main door, crossed the lobby, saw them, and turned towards their table by the bar. He was still as fascinated by her slenderness and the suppleness of her movements as he had been the first night he had met her.

'You've been for a long walk,' Graham said.

'I climbed up to the mosque to see the sunset.' She spoke in the dull tones of someone reading out the report of a funeral. 'The villagers say it's supposed to bring luck.' She avoided Graham's eyes. For the last two days he had known that the concord between them had somehow been broken.

'Did you make a wish?'

'Yes. But it won't come true if I tell you,' Vicky said. 'It's awfully stuffy in here. Can't we sit outside?'

'I once wrote a script about a wishing-well,' Cole said as they wandered out on to the terrace. 'Five different people made a wish, and every wish came true, and all five of them were perfectly miserable. In fact, I'm not at all sure that one man didn't kill himself.'

'It sounds first-class box-office,' Graham said.

'It was – unfortunately I couldn't get the studio to see it that way. But to return to our location problem . . .'

Shouts and screams of excitement came from the garden below where the children were playing. Vicky walked across to the rail beside the flood-lit pool, leaned down and began speaking in French. Presently she searched in her bag and threw down some money.

'What were you saying?' Cole asked when she rejoined them.

'I was bribing them to go away. I can't bear the noise.'

Cole glanced at her and smiled, then resumed his conversation with Graham. Vicky sat twisting the bracelets on her wrist as she gazed at the urns of cacti set on white pilasters at the end of the terrace, and the neat pots of geraniums. Suddenly she rose from the table.

'I'm going up to our room,' she announced. 'I may change and have a swim.'

'Remember to take out your contact lenses,' Graham said.

'Don't worry. I will,' Vicky called out as she moved briskly across the terrace.

Graham turned back to Cole. 'Vicky lost a lense last night,' he explained, 'and it took us two hours to find it . . . I wish to God she'd wear spectacles. But somehow with glasses she feels she's not seeing life whole. She feels ugly and deprived. It's all part of her refusal to face up to reality.'

Cole raised his head as if he were going to utter an important judgement, and changed his mind. He took an almond from a bowl of nuts, began nibbling at it, and noticed a chromium cigarette-lighter lying beside the bowl. He picked it up and handed it to Graham.

'Bangles has left her lighter behind,' Cole said.

'Thanks.'

Two children were splashing in the pool, and on the green table by the dining-room an elderly German was playing ping-pong with his daughter.

'What about a drink?' Cole asked.

Graham pushed back his chair. 'I think I'll go up and have a shower.'

Cole's voice was unusually gentle when he spoke. 'You know, she's not just going to disappear into thin air.'

Graham tried to smile. 'I dare say,' he said and left the terrace.

Vicky was lying fully dressed on her bed beneath the broad window which looked out on to the valley. Clothes from her suitcase had been thrown in an untidy heap on the wooden boards between the two beds. The room reeked of eau-de-Cologne.

'Aren't you going to swim?' Graham asked.

'I decided not to, after all.'

She took up a detective novel she had been reading and turned over the pages to find her place. Graham stripped off his bush-shirt and walked into the bathroom. He was under the shower when he heard the telephone ring. He

142

tucked a towel round his waist and came back into their room as Vicky put down the receiver.

'Who was that?' he asked.

'The hall-porter.'

'What did he want?'

'Nothing wildly important.'

'He must have phoned about something.'

'Only to say that I'd left my lighter on the terrace.'

Graham crossed the room, took the lighter from the pocket of his shirt and handed it to her. Vicky held the lighter in her hand and stared at it in silence. From below they could hear children shrieking with joy as they splashed in the pool, disturbing the gentle rap of the ball on the ping-pong table and the continuous faint hiss of the waterfall at the end of the valley. Vicky looked up at Graham with child-like, hurt eyes.

'Do you realize that Arab hotels up here only cost three-and-a-half dirhams a day?' she said. 'That's less than six shillings.'

Graham then realized that this was her method of telling him that Hamido was in Chauen. Anger surged in him. They stood facing each other. Graham had a sudden vision of Hamido's wide shoulders and blunt fingers.

'I'm sorry,' Vicky said. 'But I can't help it. Honestly I can't. You see, he's as much in love with me as you are. He's even paying his own hotel bill.'

Graham could feel the blood hot under his skin. 'Then why don't you go and stay with him?' he asked. His hand jerked in a spasm of fury. 'Look,' he said, 'you seem intent on ruining your own life – don't try to ruin mine.'

He threw open the doors of the cupboard and took out a wallet from the pocket of his linen coat. His fingers were trembling as he drew out a hundred-dirham note and handed it to her.

'That ought to keep you and your lover for at least a fortnight – at his rate.'

Vicky flinched as he thrust the note into her hand. She turned away and put down the note on the table beneath the window.

'I don't need your money, Graham.'

'Go on, take it. You'll need every penny you can lay hands on to keep your boy-friend sweet.'

Vicky moved towards the door of their bedroom and then turned. 'Do you know what you're doing?'

'I do,' Graham said.

'You realize that I won't come back to you?'

Graham stared at her without speaking.

'You do realize?' Her hand was gripping the door-handle.

'I'll be at the Ketama Hotel if you need me,' Graham said. 'It's fifty miles farther into the mountains.'

But the door had already closed behind her.

The sun had dipped behind the mountain, and a sharp bord, his head reeling, but. The head of his burnous was driving his flock down a track that led towards the village. He and the neck of each cow was a small bell that rang and tinkled in the cool evening air.

12

THE road from Chauen to Ketama lay through desolate country as wild and craggy as the Scottish Highlands, through long barren stretches of hills dappled with clumps of palmetto grass, past little green villages sprinkled with roughly-thatched cottages. Inexorably, it seemed, the road, cut into the steep face of the rock, rose higher. On one side was the lowering rock-face; on the other a drop of a thousand feet.

Towards sunset, on the evening of their arrival, Graham and Cole stood examining a plain cottage with stone walls. Beyond them, the mountains of the Rif stretched blue and red and purple in the distance.

'You know, Abdel Krim must have been quite a man,' Graham said. 'When you think that he came from this tiny cottage in this remote little village. He had no education, no training. And yet as late as 1926 with a handful of wild tribesmen and no modern weapons he held up three separate expeditionary forces.'

'Led and manned by Europeans,' Cole added.

Graham was gazing at the mountainside dotted with grey *douars* to the west of them – small family clusters of flat, mud-built houses, girt with a straggling hedge of prickly-pear. Suddenly he turned to Cole.

'Do you think I was right?' he asked quietly.

Cole looked up towards the mountain beside them, stretching to the sky like a crumpled blanket.

'I don't think you were wholly right – or wrong,' Cole

said. 'You've been led a dance, but it was your tune. She's very young. So she's even more lost than you are.'

The sun had dipped behind the mountain, and a shepherd, his head partly hidden in the hood of his burnous, was driving his flock down the track that led towards the village. Round the neck of each goat was a small bell that rattled and tinkled in the crisp evening air.

'You know,' Cole said, 'there's so little love in the world that I think one should take what one can get . . . What one gets may be hell. But some people go through their lives without finding one single bit of it.'

'But I've had love,' Graham said in protest. 'Even since my marriage broke up, I've had all the love in the world.'

Cole kicked a pebble at his feet.

'No,' he said. 'You haven't. You've had sex. You're enormously attractive to women, and you know it. So for the last twenty years you've had a series of more or less satisfactory affairs. But don't mention the word "love", because before you met Vicky I'd begun to doubt if you hadn't forgotten the meaning of the word.'

A ragged boy passed by them, hurling stones at the black goats to keep them moving.

'You mustn't ask for too much,' Cole said. 'There's two of you – both lost and both imperfect.'

He raised his arms to the sky in a gesture of despair.

'Oh God, I could write this scene so easily!' he cried. 'How simple to see your friends' mistakes! You couple of fools! Why should you expect to achieve what Adam and Eve lost? Can't you see? You're two little deformed molecules. So if you can join up and *love* – even for a while – then at least your lives may take on some shape. But it's not easy. When it first began in that Garden, when everything was still sweetness and light, there was no need for understanding, because it was all instinctive. There was no jealousy, no anger, no desire to destroy, and I dare say the lion could lie down with the lamb.'

Cole looked down at the purple valley.

'There was complete security,' he said. 'But the serpent put paid to all that. When the serpent persuaded Adam and Eve to eat the apple, he destroyed innocence. He showed them the meaning of power. "You shall be like gods," he said to them. I may say I'm quoting his very words. And both of them seized at the chance. They couldn't wait to swallow that fruit. And from that moment peace fled, and the struggle for power started.'

The crest of the mountain was now sharp against the deep blue sky.

'There's darkness and rats now in the Garden of Eden,' Cole said. 'Our instinct is no longer any good. We can't trust the compass. It doesn't point in the right direction. So we people in the wilderness have to make a frantic effort to *understand* each other. But I'm certain of this, if I'm certain of anything. To understand is to love.'

Behind the square spectacles Cole's worn grey eyes were solemn, and there was a slight harshness in his voice as he spoke.

'You asked me what I thought, Graham. And I told you. Well, I've changed my mind. I think on the balance you were wrong.'

For an instant, the sharp voice and the uncompromising verdict irritated Graham.

'What about *your* life?' he asked with a spurt of annoyance.

As soon as Graham saw the lines deepen on Cole's face he regretted his remark.

'There's not much hope for me now in my garden,' Cole said. 'But I suppose there was a chance at one stage or other. I'd have liked to have married and had children so I could watch them growing up.'

His eyes held no reproach as he gazed steadily at Graham in the fading light. Then he hunched up his shoulders in a grotesque shiver and chuckled. 'Come on. Let's go back,' he said. 'It's getting cold.'

13

THE sun had melted the surface of the Chauen road, and the double tyres of the heavy truck in front of him left a pattern on the asphalt. Graham overtook the truck and accelerated along the hill into the town. The narrow street in the shadow of the ruined castle was blocked by a herd of ewes, and he stopped the car. A young shepherd ran in pursuit of a lamb that had strayed into a side-alley and grinned slyly at him as he returned carrying it in his arms.

Neither Cole nor Graham had mentioned Vicky's name during the last days at Ketama, and now, faced with a possible meeting, Graham wondered what his reaction would be. He had begun to hope that the obsession of his love had lifted. But while he was parking the car under the shade of a large tree in the cobbled square, his eyes involuntarily searched for her. He knew, then, that he wanted to see her desperately, but from his five days without her he retained enough detachment to appreciate that it would be foolish to try to persuade her to come back.

The hall-porter recognized the car and came towards them. He shook Graham's hand and then kissed his own right forefinger in Berber greeting.

'Welcome back to Chauen, sir,' he said.

Graham resisted an impulse to ask him if he had heard any news of Vicky. The man stood erect by the car, his gnarled dishonest face creased in a smile. Graham pressed a dirham into his hand.

'How many days do you stay this time, sir?'

'Only one night. We'll be leaving for Tangier about ten

tomorrow morning. We're invited to the Pasha's house this evening, so we shan't be in the hotel for dinner.'

'How long does that tea-garden down the road stay open?' Cole asked him, as Graham unlocked the boot.

'Until two or three, sir. Sometimes it stay open all night.'

'Thanks,' Cole said.

The hall-porter moved off towards the hotel with their two cases.

'I thought we might drop in there after dinner with the Pasha,' Cole said. 'The garden looks enchanting.'

'*You* drop in.'

'Won't you come too?'

'By then I shall be limp with exhaustion, and I can't abide mint tea.'

'Isn't that strange now? I find it simply delicious.'

14

GRAHAM lay in bed, trying to concentrate on a turgid history of Morocco that the Pasha had kindly insisted on lending him. Though he had been given a different room, the décor was the same, and his eyes kept wandering along the row of bolts projecting from the thick beam fixed to the wall. Rain had fallen during the week, and the roar of the waterfall sounded louder. Suddenly there was a knock at the door.

'It's me,' Cole's voice said. 'Can I come in?'

'Please.'

As Cole came in, Graham sat up in bed. He knew instinctively that he would hear news of Vicky.

'I saw your light was on, so I thought I must pay you a visit on my way to bed,' Cole said, sitting down in the arm-chair by the window. 'I've discovered some information I think you ought to know.'

Graham handed Cole a cigarette from the tin that lay on his bed-side table and took one himself. Cole settled himself in the arm-chair and began talking. The story he had to tell was essentially simple. It began at the moment that Graham had dropped him at the tea-garden on their way back from dinner with the Pasha. . . .

The night was sultry, and most of the tables beside the sprawling almond-trees were full. Cole was sitting in the corner of the garden listening to an old man playing on a primitive one-stringed instrument called a *gnibri*, when he became aware that someone was speaking to him.

'Good evening, Mister.'

He looked up. A tall Moroccan lout with a pock-marked face was standing in front of him.

'Good evening, Mister,' the youth repeated. 'How's tricks?'

The strident voice, the thick wide lips, the knowing smirk and the tufts of black hair bursting from the open collar of his stained shirt – Cole recognized him now. It was Ibrahim, the one they called 'the donkey', Hamido's friend from the Tangier beach. He lurched into a chair opposite Cole and grinned stupidly. The cigarette in his hand trembled as he held it to his lips, and his breath stank of alcohol.

'Will you have a mint tea?' Cole asked politely.

Ibrahim shook his head, and his whole body jerked like a puppet. 'There is beer. You can find beer if you know how.' He spoke slowly and assertively. 'Do you want beer?'

'No,' Cole said. 'I haven't tried the mint tea yet.'

A nervous-looking waiter sidled towards their table, and Ibrahim gave him loud orders.

'You are not any more with the English girl,' Ibrahim said as the waiter crept away.

'Why do you say that?'

Ibrahim shrugged and parted his lips in a grin. Cole noticed that his teeth were decayed.

'How is it that I know the English girl is no more with you?' Ibrahim asked. 'I think you would like to find out.'

'I would,' Cole agreed.

'But you cannot find out unless I tell you. And Ibrahim may not want to tell you . . . Ibrahim does not like to be insulted.'

152

'Who's insulted you?'

'I am told to give him a message, and then I am insulted.'

Ibraham's cigarette dropped from his fingers on to the grass. Cole gave him another.

'Who did you have to give a message to? Hamido?'

Ibrahim's dull eyes seemed to focus for a moment. 'Yes, to Hamido. But he insulted me, and I do not like to be insulted.'

'Who was the message from?'

'From the American woman. Hamido's friend. The big woman in Tangier with the villa on the Marshan.'

Ibrahim stopped as the waiter came up to the table with a mint tea and two bottles of beer.

'Open the beer,' Ibrahim said. 'Both bottles. That is good. And now you may go.'

Ibrahim took a long gulp, tilting back his head.

'I am her friend for one year when I am sixteen,' he said. 'But then Hamido came along, and I am forgotten. But two days ago she send for me and she give me to drink and she give me money – plenty money – because she is very rich. She has a big white car and a big nose.'

Ibrahim poured some more beer into his glass.

'She has found out that Hamido has been going with the English girl,' he said. 'And she is very angry. Before you leave Tangier she send for Hamido one night and she scream at him and say she will give him no more money and no more presents. But when she is no more angry, I tell her Hamido has gone to Chauen. And she tell me that I must go up to Chauen.'

Ibrahim was silent. Cole sipped his mint tea. 'Why must you go to Chauen?' he asked.

'I must go to find Hamido, and I must tell him he must come back to Tangier. I must tell him she has a big present that wait for him. When I ask her how much, she say one hundred dollar. Before, she has given him good presents, but never more than twenty dollar.'

Ibrahim stifled a belch and stretched out his hand for the second bottle.

'So I came here to Chauen,' he said. 'And I find Hamido. He is in a hotel with the English girl. But I tell him I must talk with him, so I take him to a bar and I buy him plenty to drink with the money the American woman has given me. And then I tell him he is okay with the American woman and he must be going back to Tangier tomorrow because she is good with him and give him presents like the cigarette-lighter he has that is all gold. And I tell Hamido that the American woman is always living in Tangier but the English girl will go back to London and leave him. "So why do you waste your time with her?" I ask him. And he say to me, "because I love her", and I say to him, "but you love one hundred dollar also", and he laugh and say "it is not the same thing". And he say that the English girl will not go back to London, she will stay in Morocco, and one day he will take her to see his mother in Fez.'

Ibrahim gazed at the froth of the beer he had poured out spilling over the rim of the glass.

'I say to him, "why you think the English girl will stay in Morocco?" and he say, "because she love me", and I say "if she love you, why she no give you presents like the American woman? Why has she not give you the gold watch in Hakim's window?" And he say nothing, so we have more to drink, and I say to him, "the English girl will leave you and in London she will forget you", and he say, "if I ask her to stay in Morocco, she will stay". And I tell him, "no, she will go back", and he say, "no, she will stay". So then Hamido say, "very good, we

154

will ask her". So we have more drinks and go back to the hotel.'

'Which hotel?' Cole asked.

'The Mabrouk. It is near the *souk*, the market. . . . So we go back. . . .'

As Ibrahim's words dropped like pebbles from his heavy lips, Cole could envisage the scene. He could see the bedroom of the Arab hotel with the large double mattress covered with a greasy red quilt in the corner where Vicky sat propped up against a few worn cushions. The whitewashed walls and the narrow window with its blue-painted sill, the cracked ewer, and the soap-dish on the chipped washstand – he could see it all. . . .

Vicky put down the magazine she was reading as Hamido came in followed by Ibrahim.

'Hello, Vicky,' Hamido said. 'We have come back.' He crossed the room and leaned heavily against the washstand while Ibrahim stood swaying gently by the door.

'We have come back,' Hamido repeated, 'because I have a question I must ask you – a very important question.'

'You've drunk too much,' Vicky said crisply. 'Both of you.'

'We have drunk,' Hamido said, 'because we have had important matters to talk over. And the question is this. Will you stay in Morocco?'

Vicky was puzzled. 'I'll be staying till the end of my holiday,' she said.

'Can you stay longer?'

'Not really. I've got a job in England.'

Ibrahim nodded his head towards Hamido and smirked. 'You see,' he said to him. 'I have told you this.'

'But if I ask you to stay,' Hamido said to Vicky, 'if I tell you I am loving you very much, if I tell you I need you to stay with me, then you will stay – yes?'

Vicky was annoyed with Hamido for being drunk and she resented Ibrahim's arrogant leer.

'What's the point of the question?' she asked.

Hamido picked up the lid of the soap-dish and flicked it with his finger.

'Will you stay?' he repeated.

'I've asked you to tell me the point of the question.'

Ibrahim, who was now leaning his shoulder against the wall, gave a loud, drunken laugh.

'I can tell you the point of the question,' he said. 'Hamido wants to know if he must go back to the fat American woman in Tangier who pays him money.'

Hamido sprang from the washstand, knocking the ewer of water on to the floor. His hands were shaking.

'Get out!' Hamido cried in a shrill scream. 'Get out or I'll kill you.'

Ibrahim backed away from him, opened the door in one movement, and rushed down the stairs. From the bottom of the staircase he called out the taunts that came into his mind, and heard Hamido slam the bedroom door. Ibrahim had then visited a bar to restore his self-respect – and then another. And he had ended his jaunt by visiting the tea-garden – a shambling, drunken lout who gaped dazedly at Cole across the table. . . .

'And that's all I could find out from the boy,' Cole said in conclusion.

Graham brushed away some ash that had fallen on to the sheet.

156

'I thought I should tell you,' Cole continued, 'in case you feel we ought to do something about it.'

'Such as?'

'Go round to the hotel and try to make her see sense.'

Graham shook his head.

'One sure way to make her stay with Hamido is for us to make any attempt to persuade her away from him,' he said. 'Vicky's got to make her own decision.' He felt he was beginning to learn at last.

'They're so excitable. Do you think she's safe with him?'

'I doubt it,' Graham replied. 'But that's a risk we've got to take. There's nothing we can do except hope that she'll see reason in time.'

15

GRAHAM recognized the Berber maid who was standing in the corridor and stopped to give her some money because he had forgotten to tip her when he left for Ketama.

'Barraklaufik, moosoo,' she said. 'Thank you, sir.'

The young receptionist was on the terrace watching the pool being filled with fresh water pumped in by the fire-brigade.

'You should stay longer with us, Mr Hadley,' he said.

He's right, Graham thought, smiling back at him. Mr Hadley should be staying longer. He should stay until he can collect his girl and bring her safely with him back to Tangier.

'Any messages for me this morning?' Graham asked.

'None, sir.'

Cole came down the stairs wearing the tight gaberdine suit he had had made by a Spanish tailor in Tangier.

'Are we all set to leave?' he asked.

Graham hesitated. There was still time to change his mind, and Cole would understand. Perhaps he should ask the way to the Hotel Mabrouk and go round to see her – he need only stay a few minutes – just to make sure . . . Perhaps . . .

'All set,' Graham said. 'Let's go.'

They followed the hall-porter across the cobbled square towards the tree under which they had left the Chevrolet. Then, for a moment, Graham stopped. Though he could only see a section of her face and a part of her arm because she was sitting crouched on her suitcase at the far side of

158

the car, he recognized her immediately. As they approached, she got up from her old suitcase and stood beside the car, and he saw that she had been beaten up. Her hair was dishevelled and her cheek was bruised, and there was a cut on the corner of her mouth. In silence she stared at Graham with the wounded expression in her eyes that he knew so well. But this time the child had really been hurt. Her hands were trembling slightly, and the reason she did not speak was because she could not trust her voice.

Graham opened the near-side door of the car.

'Get in,' he said quietly.

Vicky glanced up at him for an instant, then moved into the front seat. Cole picked up her suitcase, put it in the boot with their two cases, and tipped the hall-porter, who was looking on with his dishonest grin. In silence Graham drove out of the square and down the steep, narrow street, past the chemist shop and the flamboyant posters outside the tiny local cinema, through the Spanish-built quarter on the outskirts of the village with its trim avenues and neat gardens, and out on to the dusty track that led towards the main road to Tangier. When Cole began to shift uneasily in the back, Graham knew that he was preparing to break the tension.

'Well, Bangles,' Cole said. 'It's fine to see you again.' It was not one of Cole's most inspired lines of dialogue, Graham decided. But it seemed to work, for Vicky turned back to him, and her lips wavered in a smile.

They turned a bend round a shoulder of the mountain – and there, in the road ahead of them, stood a young man wearing grey jeans and a torn purple shirt unbuttoned so that it showed a wide expanse of chest. Matted curls fell over a grimy swollen face, and it was only when the car drew closer that Graham recognized Hamido. As the car approached him, Hamido stepped from the verge into the centre of the dusty asphalt and flung out his arms wide, blocking the narrow road. Graham neither braked nor accelerated. He forced his hands and foot to remain fixed in position. Without deviating, the heavy car moved at speed along the road, heading straight for the boy.

'Graham! For God's sake!' But it was too late for him, now, to change his decision. His hands on the wheel and his foot on the pedal were rigid, as if they had been locked in position by his previous act of volition. And for a second it seemed to him that through the wind-screen the boy's eyes met his once again and locked, and at that instant of time, as the car bore down on Hamido, Graham believed that the boy must have perceived the warning behind the staring eyes that opposed him, for at the last moment, when it seemed inevitable that the black car would sweep over him, the boy sprang aside and leaped clear.

Graham spoke to Vicky.

'Don't look back.' His voice was harsh and commanding.

Vicky did not turn. In the driving-mirror Graham could see the boy's chest rising and falling and his face puckered with frustration and grief. He saw him brush his brow with the back of his hand. Then Hamido stooped down and picked up a stone and hurled it after the car in a futile gesture of impotence.

At the next corner Graham looked back. Hamido was standing in the road, his shoulders drooping, his hands limp by his side, watching the car disappear into the distance.

16

THE landlady had hung some early-nineteenth-century aquarelles of Morocco on the walls, and the round-faced Fatima had filled the living-room with tuberoses. As a result Graham had found the flat less impersonal since their return. He glanced across at Vicky, who was sitting in an arm-chair with her head tilted back, her eyes closed, and her face completely covered in cold cream.

'I'm sure it doesn't do you the slightest good,' he said.

Her eyelids blinked. 'I can't argue with you at the moment,' she said without moving her mouth. 'But it does. Are my fifteen minutes up?'

'All but thirty seconds.'

Vicky reached out for the packet of tissues on the arm of the chair and began removing the cream, tossing the crumpled pieces of used paper into the fireplace. Graham picked up the waste-paper basket and put it down beside her. She looked up and grinned. He moved behind her chair and slid his fingers between the smooth leather and her back. He watched her fold a tissue into four and begin to clean her nails.

'Have you thought what we're going to do when we get back to London?' He had rehearsed the question several times, carefully selecting the word 'we'.

For a while she was motionless. 'I suppose I'll go back to the flat and dear old Muriel.'

'But there is an alternative.'

'I know.' She fumbled beside her and produced a bottle in which he could see a small brush.

'Why shouldn't you move into my flat?'

He caught the pungent smell of the varnish as she opened the bottle. He splayed out his fingers against her back.

'It would be difficult,' she said, and he knew from the tone of her voice that she had thought out her answer as carefully as he had rehearsed his question.

'Muriel wouldn't be able to pay for the flat by herself, and I couldn't opt out – just like that. And then there's the problem of my parents. If they came up to town to see me, I'd have a lot of explaining to do when they laid eyes on your flat.' Vicky blew on a nail she had been painting. 'I could hardly tell them that I'd bought the Utrillo and the Steinway on hire purchase.'

Graham laughed.

'Then leave a few things at your old flat, and we'll still pay your share of the rent. And that'll satisfy both Muriel and your parents.'

Vicky held out her shiny wet nails for inspection and then lifted herself from the chair with her elbows.

'That sounds all right to me, but I'll have to discuss it with Muriel and get her on our side, because if my Ma rings up, she'll have to have a story ready.'

Vicky crossed to the window with her arms outstretched like a sleepwalker and looked down. Suddenly Graham was afraid that Hamido might be waiting, hunched up in his old position on the wall opposite. As he joined Vicky at the window he sensed that she had understood the cause for his alarm. They gazed together into the empty street.

'Did you know that Cole met Ibrahim in Chauen?' he asked.

'No.'

'He told Cole he'd been to see you at the Hotel Mabrouk.'

'So I suppose you weren't surprised to see me the next morning.'

Graham turned from the window so that he could see her face. The cut on her mouth had almost healed, but there was still a mark where she had been bruised. 'I nearly came round to your hotel that morning.'

She smiled at him. 'It was just as well you didn't.'

He held her chin for a moment with his fingers.

'What *did* happen after Ibrahim left?' he asked.

Vicky stared at a mule-drawn water-cart that was passing by with a group of children tripping behind it taunting the old driver.

'Did you know that Ibrahim had made the mistake of blurting out that Hamido was kept by an American woman? Well, when he came out with that, Hamido went into a frenzy. He flew at him, and Ibrahim rushed off down the stairs. They were both drunk, and their whole behaviour gave me an awful feeling of being a stranger – an outsider who could never belong to their world. When we were alone together, I could accept Hamido and he could accept me. But the moment he was with his friends we seemed to reject each other. That evening was typical of it. Ibrahim started shouting in Arabic from downstairs, and Hamido slammed the door.

'I picked up the ewer of water that he'd knocked over in his excitement and mopped up the water with a towel. When I looked up, Hamido was staring at me blearily. It was rather frightening. He was very pale, and I could tell from the set of his cheek-bones that his teeth were clenched.

'"Why must you leave me and go to England?" he asked.

'"Because I have to work," I said. "I have to go back to my job."

'"But I have asked you," he said. "So now you must stay."

163

'"I'm sorry," I said. "But for lots of reasons I've got to go back."

'He looked at me with his sad eyes and shook his head. "You do not love me," he said, "now that you know I have been with the American woman." And he began to weep. "Please don't go," he said. "If you stay we can open a beach-bar and work together. And if you stay I will not have to go back to the American woman."

'Suddenly it all seemed very squalid. I looked round the dingy little room, and then I looked at Hamido. I was angry and I wanted to hurt him, so I said, "I suppose it's easier to be kept by me than by her."

'The tears stopped and he gaped at me. And the next thing I knew he was hitting me. The odd thing is I felt nothing at all – I was dazed, I expect. I could feel the blood trickling down my chin, but there was no pain. When he'd finished we stood looking at each other for a moment. Then he gave a wild scream, like an animal caught in a trap, and ran out of the room.

'I locked the door. It was only when I began to bathe my face that the pain started. I went to bed, and somehow I slept. When I woke up it was dawn. I looked outside the door in case Hamido was asleep in the passage, but there was no one. So I packed my case and went downstairs to settle the bill with the proprietor. It came to very little.

'Then I walked towards the square opposite the Hotel Chauen. I wanted to find a taxi and drive in it to Tangier. But in the square I saw the old Chevrolet parked under that huge tree.'

Vicky paused and glanced up at him.

'I was amazed because I thought you'd be in Ketama for at least a week. I didn't want to go into the hotel, so I sat by the car until you came out.'

Vicky sighed. 'And you saw the next instalment for yourself.'

Graham stretched out his arm. 'Is the varnish dry?' he asked. She nodded and he took her hand. 'You know we were talking about your dreary job?' he said. 'I think we might find you something at the studio in the script department. You'd probably find that more interesting.'

'Sounds fine,' she said absently. Graham watched her as her eyes wandered along the street leading into the main boulevard, and moved towards the low wall in front of the house opposite and crossed to the little garden in the centre of the roundabout, as if she were taking in a last impression to register on her memory. In the garden the children were grouped in a circle to play their game.

> 'Chérie, je t'aime,
> Chérie, je t'adore,
> Come la salsa,
> Del pomodore. . . .'

'Shall I tell you something?' Vicky asked.

'Please.'

'Even when I was with Hamido . . . I couldn't believe it was all over between us.'

Her face turned slowly from the window.

'You see, I kept thinking about you,' she said.

PART THREE

1

THE keyboard distracted him, and Graham closed the lid of the piano as he passed.

'And the subject has universal appeal,' he said. 'Paragraph.'

Betty turned over a page of her shorthand notebook and looked up. He knew from her face that she had been almost as disturbed by the news from Los Angeles as he had.

'I am sure that you and your fellow-directors will appreciate,' he continued, 'that the screen-play I am enclosing is only a first draft. Full stop. But I am also sure that you will agree that it is one of the finest jobs of work that Cole Edwards has done. Full stop. With best wishes. Yours sincerely . . . And that's to Bob Rayburn at Anglo-Associated.'

Betty stood up and brushed her pleated skirt with her hand.

'Will you get that typed out tonight and I'll sign it,' Graham said. 'And could you be an angel and drop it in at Wardour Street on your way home? Take a taxi, of course.'

'Right you are, Mr Hadley.' Betty fastened the page with a rubber band and inserted her pencil into the side of the pad and beamed at him in condolence. 'I must say I find it all most upsetting,' she said. 'But I suppose one just can't rely on foreigners.'

Graham rested his knee on the piano stool. Betty still lingered by the door, and he knew that she expected him to make some pronouncement on the disaster.

169

G

'It's annoying,' he said, 'but it was to be expected. I should have seen the writing on the wall as soon as I got that stalling letter from Wainwright. Obviously as soon as they heard that Paramount weren't interested they got cold feet. If Anglo-Associated will play we've no problem. Otherwise our only hope is to rely on the French backers for the whole amount.'

'I still think it's rotten luck,' Betty said.

The doorbell rang and he moved towards the hall and then remembered that Mrs Lucas was in the flat.

'It'll teach me never to try to do without a producer again,' Graham said.

'Well, I'll run along to your study and get this typed,' Betty said brightly.

As she tripped out of the room she met Cole coming in.

'Good evening, Mr Edwards.'

Cole gave her a flirtatious wink. 'And how's Mata Hari this evening?'

'No better for being teased,' Betty replied, tossing her head coyly as she left the room.

'Well?' Cole asked.

'I've just dictated the letter to Anglo on the lines we discussed,' Graham said. 'Let's hope it does the trick. I'll give them a week and then I'll have to fly to Paris.'

'Are you letting the French boys know yet?'

'Not till I've found out the form with Anglo.'

'That sounds wise.'

Graham gathered together the files that were lying open on the sofa. 'Anyway,' he said, 'we've been talking about nothing else all day, so let's steer clear of it tonight. Scotch-and-soda?'

'Please,' Cole said. 'And where's Vicky?'

'She's not back yet. This is one of the days she goes down

to the studio. You knew I'd got her a job with them working on that Jean Chaume play they're hoping to film?'

'So I heard. That was very adroit of you, wasn't it?'

'It won't last long. But it's a start anyhow.'

'And how are things going at home?'

Graham handed Cole his drink.

'Fine,' he said. 'At first I thought I might have a little trouble with Mrs Lucas. But she took it all in her stride. I suspect she was getting a little bored with just looking after a lone bachelor. I was afraid she'd be shocked. But she's taken quite a shine to Vicky. In a way it's fortunate that Vicky's so hopelessly incapable of looking after herself or anyone else, because I'm sure that if she'd tried to do anything helpful around the flat, Mrs Lucas would have declared war.'

Cole leaned forward and took a lump of ice from the bucket on the table.

'Any news of Hamido?' he asked. 'I keep having nightmares about him standing in the middle of the road. And Vicky's also managed to invade my dreams. I woke up the other morning firmly convinced that I'd got two blue contact lenses in one eye and a threepenny-bit in the other.'

'If you remember,' Graham said, 'you advised me not to discuss Hamido with her. And in fact neither of us even mentioned his name until a few days ago.'

Mrs Lucas knocked and peered cautiously round the door. She looked poker-faced, Graham noticed, so probably Betty had told her the news of the Abdel Krim film over a cup of coffee in the kitchen.

'What time do you want dinner, Mr Hadley?' she asked.

Graham glanced at his watch. 'Miss Tollard should be here at any moment. So shall we say in about half an hour?'

171

The door shut silently. 'We were talking about Hamido,' Cole said.

'Hamido,' Graham repeated the name. He had seen the letter as he sorted out the mail. On the back of the envelope was written: 'Expeditrice: Evelyn Roper, La Ronde Bar, Tangier.'

'Vicky had a letter from him the other day,' Graham said. It was easy to talk to Cole about it because he was fond of him and because he remembered the scene so vividly.

'There's a letter for you, Vicky,' he had said. He knew that there were very few things that would get her out of bed and a letter was one of them. One morning when she was late for her work and still lingering in bed he had tried it out as a joke, but he had been sorry when he had seen the disappointment in her face.

So she had come into the living-room and he had handed her the letter. She had been standing in her dressing-gown by the piano as she read through it.

'What's Evelyn got to say?' he had asked.

Vicky folded the letter and put it back in the envelope. 'It's not from Evelyn,' she said. 'It's from Hamido.'

'How did he have this address? You must have written to him.'

Vicky slid the envelope into the pocket of her dressing-gown. 'I did write to him,' she said. 'I had a letter from him about a month ago. He'd sent it to the Earl's Court address. It was such a pathetic letter that I felt I simply must answer it.'

'But how is Evelyn mixed up in all this?'

'Because Hamido's letter ended up with him begging me to reply, but – typically enough – he'd forgotten to give an address. So I wrote to Evelyn enclosing the letter for him and asking her to give it to him.'

172

'She won't have thanked you for that.'

'No, I suppose not.'

Graham had hoped that Vicky might tell him what Hamido had written, but she did not refer to it again. The following day he had seen the torn pieces of the letter lying at the bottom of a waste-paper basket, and for a moment he had been tempted to pick out the fragments.

'But in the end I left them untouched,' Graham concluded.

Cole put down his glass. 'That was very noble of you,' he said.

Betty came in with his letter to Bob Rayburn and Graham checked and signed it. He handed the top copy to Cole and put the carbon on top of the stack of files.

'Reads well to me,' Cole said, giving the letter back to Betty. 'By the way, did you think of approaching George Benon? He's closely tied up with Anglo.'

'I thought about it,' Graham said, waving good-bye to Betty as she left the room. 'But he's invited me to dine with him this Monday, so I thought I'd broach it then.' He picked up Cole's empty glass and walked across to the drink-tray. 'I can't think what's happened to Vicky,' he said. 'Do you have that terrible fear whenever somebody's late? You know – that they're dead? I suppose it comes from the war. I've tried to explain it to Vicky, but she just can't understand. She's invariably late herself and never expects anyone else to be on time.'

'Good night, Mr Hadley; good night, Mr Edwards.' Betty's voice from the hall sounded resolutely cheerful. They could hear her having a whispered conversation with Mrs Lucas and then her bright 'Cheerio, Mrs L.' and the door slamming.

'I keep asking Vicky to telephone if she's going to be late,' Graham said. 'But she never does.'

173

'Vicky's careless by nature,' Cole said.

'I think that at last she's beginning to rely on me just a little,' Graham said. 'But she's terribly independent. I suppose it comes from living on her own in town. Do you know, she won't take a penny from me? After hours of persuasion she finally agreed to let me buy her a new dress. I expect she'll wear it at the Benons on Monday. I told her that in the celluloid world we inhabit we have to look rich even if we *are* broke. But it's very odd. I happen to know she's being paid quite well for the work she's been doing for the studio, but she hoards her money like a squirrel.'

'I expect it's all part of her insecurity.'

Graham took the carbon copy of his letter to Anglo-Associated and put it inside the cover of the top file.

'My insecurity's going to be quite phenomenal if Bob Rayburn doesn't like our script,' he said, as the bell rang in the hall.

'Let's try not to think about it,' Cole replied.

In the hall they could hear Vicky's voice. 'I'm so sorry to have to ring. But I left my key behind again.'

'That's all right, dear.' Mrs Lucas's voice was as placid as usual. 'If you'd remembered to take it, you'd probably have lost it.'

The door of the living-room swung open and Vicky came in. 'Sorry I'm so desperately late,' she said. 'But I stopped by to see Muriel on the way back and she kept me talking – we hardly ever see each other these days – and then I had to wait for ages in a bus queue.'

'Why didn't you take a taxi?' Graham asked.

'Because I'm economizing.'

'Whatever for?'

'I'm saving up to buy myself a car.'

'So that's where your salary's been going to,' Graham said. He noticed that her face was slightly flushed and she seemed out of breath. Perhaps she had run along the street from the bus-stop.

'Speaking of cars – what are you both doing this week-end?' Cole asked. 'I thought we might drive into the country while this delicious weather still lasts.'

'You two go,' Vicky said briskly. 'But I can't. I've got to go down to Larkin. I haven't seen my parents for months, and I've been feeling rather guilty about it. I thought I'd stay with them for a long week-end. I've finished my first draft of the Jean Chaume play, so I've got nothing to worry about.'

Mrs Lucas came in with a tray of cutlery to finish laying the table.

'I'm all for you seeing your parents,' Graham said. 'But will you promise to be back by seven on Monday evening?'

'Why?'

'The Benons have asked us to dine with them. And now that our American backing has fallen through, George Benon could be quite helpful.'

'Then I'll be back by seven.'

Mrs Lucas beckoned to them from the table in the raised alcove at the far end of the room.

'Dinner's served, Mr Hadley,' she announced grandly.

2

HE knew that Vicky was away, for she always lay against him like a child in her sleep, and he had missed her in the night. They usually slept in the same bed, and Vicky would move back to her own room before eight o'clock for the benefit of Mrs Lucas. Vicky preferred his bed because of the baroque headpiece – a gilt dragon sprawling across a white background with its head projecting in the centre. The dragon had originally been fierce and snarling. But in one of her nightmares Vicky had reached out and grasped at it, and in the morning they had found the head lying between them. Graham had called in a plasterer from the studio who had made a new head. But instead of looking ferocious, the dragon's expression was now bovine and timid.

The sunlight shining between the curtains had woken him. The weather was always most tempting, he thought, on a morning when he was able to dawdle in bed. He rose and wandered along the hall into the kitchen. Without Mrs Lucas bustling around, the room seemed empty. A radio was standing on top of the refrigerator and he switched it on. He recognized the irritating voice of a Sunday-morning preacher and turned the knob until he found music.

It was the first week-end he had spent without Vicky since their return from Tangier, and he had made no plans. He connected his pleasures so much with her that any expedition without her was unattractive, and he had declined Cole's invitation to drive to Arundel. The music stopped and a voice began to speak in French, and he turned it off. He looked at his watch. It was eleven o'clock. He switched on the electric kettle. He decided he would have lunch at The Lion off Curzon Street. He was almost sure to find someone he knew there. It was odd, he thought, that Vicky had not telephoned. She had left for Larkin on Friday evening. Perhaps both lines were out of order. He walked into his room and picked up the receiver of the green telephone by his bed. If he rang the number of the white telephone on the table opposite he would know that both lines were working. He dialled the number and when the bell began to ring he suddenly thought it was Vicky calling him. But then he remembered he was telephoning himself.

'I'm so sorry,' the fat man said. 'And I don't usually drink beer either.'

Graham felt the cold liquid seeping into his shirt.

'That's all right,' he said.

'I've made such a mess of your suit,' the fat man said. He took a yellow handkerchief from the pocket of his check sports jacket and began to mop Graham's shoulder. 'I don't really like the stuff. But I suppose it's one way of making friends. And now your coat's all damp. Let me get you a drink.'

Graham smiled. 'Thanks, but I'm meeting some people.' He moved away discreetly and pushed towards the bar and greeted the black-haired muscular landlady.

'Haven't seen you since that film of yours came out,' she said. 'I went to it with Frank a couple of weeks back. It was a bit above my head. Still. . . . What'll you have?'

'Vodka-and-tonic, please, Nina.'

177

Nina examined a glass and then held it under the bottle.

'What can I get you?' Graham asked.

Nina gave him a comedy wink. 'No thanks, love. I try not to take them from friends.'

'Graham!' He turned, and Larry Bates squeezed his way to the bar beside him.

'How's the film going?' Graham asked.

'Fine, fine,' Larry said. The sweat was streaming down his round, puffy face. 'Do you know my wife?' His eyes narrowed as he scanned the room. 'Sorry, but she seems to have lost herself.' Graham followed his gaze. No one he knew had ever met Larry's wife, and it was rumoured that she did not exist. Larry, it was suggested, had invented her as a useful excuse to be rid of his nymphets when they began to bore him.

'What will you drink?'

'A lager,' Larry said. 'I always drink lager on Sunday morning. By the way, your young friend Simon Tasker has been quite a success. He can act, that boy. It was a small part, but he made out all right, as I expect you've heard.'

'I'm delighted,' Graham said.

'Hasn't he rung you? The ungrateful little basket! He must have got back last Tuesday.' Larry raised the lager to his lips. 'How's your Moroccan project going?'

'Fine, fine,' Graham replied in the same off-hand confident voice that Larry had used. 'I've got Cole Edwards on the script.'

'He's a good boy. . . . Will you excuse me, Graham I must go and find my wife. . . . Are you in town this week?'

'I don't think so. I'm probably off to Paris on Tuesday.

'Then give me a tinkle when you get back, and come round one night for dinner. . . . There's my wife behind tha

178

pillar.' Larry seized his lager and began to move away. 'Thanks for the drink and don't forget to call me.'

Graham wondered if Larry had used his mythical wife as an excuse to avoid staying with him. News travelled fast in the film world, and perhaps Larry had heard that his American backing had failed him and was afraid that Graham might ask him for support.

'I'm so sorry.' He could hear the distressed apologetic voice above the chatter of the far end of the bar. He looked round. The fat man was brushing the shoulder of an elderly gentleman with his yellow handkerchief. 'I don't really like the stuff,' the fat man was saying. 'But I suppose it's one way of making friends.'

3

GRAHAM took up a bunch of newspapers, settled himself on the sofa, and turned over the pages of the *Sunday Times* until he reached the film reviews. Two columns of praise were devoted to a film called *The Ace of Clubs*. He had turned down the script of it three years earlier and now it seemed likely that the production would be a success. He was stretching out for the *Observer* to compare the reviews when he heard the doorbell. He glanced at his watch and wondered who would ring the bell of his flat at three o'clock on a Sunday afternoon. He had once lived near a London County Council Estate in St John's Wood, and every Sunday droves of children of various ages had called to ask if he wanted his car cleaned. Answering the door every other minute had annoyed him so much that he had had a spy-hole fixed into the door, but the children had overcome this defence by sticking chewing-gum over the glass. Graham rose and wandered out of the living-room just as the doorbell rang again. He opened the door.

A very slim girl was standing in the passage by the lift. She would have been attractive, he noticed, if her features had not been so strained.

'I don't suppose you were expecting me,' she said, raising her head arrogantly as she spoke.

He stared at her. The thick dark hair, the bright, close-set eyes, the swarthy complexion, the sharp, uptilted nose, the tight mouth with thin, rather sensual lips – he had seen that face before, and yet he could not place her.

He saw that her eyes veered past him through the hall
and into the flat.

'Aren't you going to ask me in?'

The carefully modulated voice and the cultivated accent
jolted his memory, and he realized that he had not recognized her because she had been wearing uniform the only
time they had met before.

'Hullo, Muriel,' he said, trying to conceal his surprise at
her visit. 'It's nice to see you. Come along in.'

'Thank you,' she said. 'I hope I haven't come at an in-
convenient moment.'

He was sure that this was the curt voice she used to the
patients in her ward at the hospital. As she rose in seniority
the curtness would probably become more pronounced.
He tried to match his voice with hers. 'Not at all. I was
just reading the papers.'

Muriel stood by the fireplace gazing round the room. He
remembered, now, that her surname was Craig.

'You've done yourself quite well here,' she said. 'No
wonder Vicky prefers it to our old flat. It's really quite
original.'

'I'm glad you like it,' Graham said. 'What can I get you
to drink?'

'It's a little early for me, thanks. But don't let me stop
you.'

She stood there motionless – like a bird of dark omen,
Graham decided as he crossed to the drink-table and
poured himself a Kümmel.

'Won't you sit down?' he said.

'Thank you.'

She sat on the edge of a white arm-chair with her legs
decorously crossed beneath her tight skirt. Self-consciously
she pulled the hem over her knees.

'You may be wondering why I've come round.'

181

'Yes,' he replied. 'I am.'

'I thought you would be,' Muriel said complacently. 'And I dare say you'll be still more surprised when you hear my reason for coming.'

Graham picked up the Adam-and-Eve box.

'Cigarette?'

'Thank you.' He noticed that her nails were short and unvarnished.

Graham lit their cigarettes before speaking. 'And what *was* your reason for coming?'

'In one word,' Muriel said, 'mercy.'

For once a line of dialogue had startled him.

'Mercy?'

'Yes. You see, in a way I'm rather sorry for you.'

The confidence in her voice disturbed him.

'Do you mind telling me why?'

'Not at all. As I've said already, that's why I'm here.'

Her dark eyes were gleaming, and he knew instinctively that she was moving towards some dramatic moment she had carefully planned. Long training had taught him that a sure way to lower the temperature of any scene was to sit down. Graham now strolled across the room and lowered himself into an arm-chair opposite her.

'I'm listening,' he said. The cigarette trembled between her fingers. Graham watched her in silence.

'I'm sorry for you,' she said, 'because I think you're a sensitive, intelligent person and I'm certain you're heading for disaster.'

'Why?'

'You're heading for disaster with Vicky.'

Her eyes were fixed on him, and suddenly Graham felt nervous. He wanted to swallow.

'What makes you think so?' he asked.

'Intuition, for a start.'

Graham smiled with relief. 'Intuition can be terribly misleading, as we all know,' he said. He was regaining confidence.

'But it's not only intuition. After all, I've shared a flat with Vicky for nearly a year, and one gets to know a person quite well under those conditions.'

'I'm sure one does,' Graham agreed.

'In fact, in some ways I expect I know Vicky better than you do.'

'Perhaps. But I doubt it.'

'I'm sure I know more about her character. For instance, I expect you'd be surprised to know how secretive she is.'

'Not a bit. She's naturally reserved, that's all.'

'No, she's secretive. She wants to know everything about you, but she doesn't want you to know too much about her.'

'Don't most people?'

'And another thing. She can't bear to be in second place. She's got to be the captain of games and the head ward-sister.' Muriel's eyes were glittering and she was breathing heavily. 'But not only does she have to *be* the top of the class and *know* more about everything in life than anyone else. She's also got to be the most attractive girl for miles around. Oh yes! No one must be allowed to be thought as alluring as Miss Victoria Tollard.'

Graham gaped at her. On their previous meeting at the flat she had given him the impression of admiring Vicky and being loyal to her, but now her voice was shaking with animosity as the words poured out. Either on that first occasion she had been acting, Graham decided, or Vicky had done something to arouse her venom.

'No young man must be allowed to look at anyone else. And if he does? If he happens to be so stupid as to prefer another girl and want to go to bed with her, what then?

Why then it must be stopped – and at any price. And what surer way of stopping it than to entice that young man into falling for Miss Tollard. So that's what happens. Time and again. But the other girl mustn't object. Oh no! She must just be pleasant and understanding about it all . . . Because Victoria Tollard has not only got a beautiful body, but a beautiful character as well. And so all must be forgiven her.' Muriel stubbed out her cigarette. 'Have you ever lain awake in bed, knowing the person you're mad about is making love with someone else in the next room? Well, I have. Sometimes in that flat with Vicky and Simon I thought I was going mad. Perhaps I have. I'd take three or four grains of sodium amytal, but it made no difference . . . However, this time Vicky's done it once too often.'

Muriel's mouth was twisted, and Graham looked away from her.

'If you've come here to poison my mind against Vicky,' he said, 'you're wasting your time and mine.'

Muriel clenched her hands together in an effort to control herself.

'I've come to open your eyes to the truth,' she said.

Graham stubbed out his cigarette in the ashtray on the table beside him and stood up.

'I'm not interested,' he said. 'I think you'd better go.'

Muriel's lips slid into a smile. 'But you *are* interested,' she said, 'and you know it. You pretend to yourself that you're shocked by me, but in fact you're quite fascinated.'

'You're wrong, I promise you.'

'You realize that I've got something important to tell you, don't you? You know that there's some hard fact I've been keeping from you. After all, I wouldn't have come round here if I'd only had intuition and my knowledge of Vicky to go on, would I? And don't pretend you don't long to find out what it's all about.'

184

'I'm not interested, I tell you.'

'You're not interested to know where Vicky Tollard is at this moment?'

'I happen to *know* where she is at this moment.'

'Where?'

'At Larkin with her parents.'

'Would you care to ring them and make certain?'

'No.'

'Why not?'

'Because I happen to trust Vicky.'

'So if I tell you that Vicky hasn't gone down to Larkin this week-end and never intended going there, you won't believe me?'

'No.' Graham's eyes searched round the room for his glass. He crossed to the marble-topped table and picked it up. The unpleasant note of conviction had come back into Muriel's voice.

'Shall I tell you where Vicky's spending this week-end? Shall I tell you? She's in a hotel six miles north of Oxford – with Simon Tasker.'

Graham kept his voice steady. 'I don't believe you.'

'I know the name of the hotel. We could get the number from directory inquiries and ring up and find out. Or shall we ring Larkin? We could get that number from directory inquiries too.'

Muriel rose from the arm-chair and stood facing him.

'You're now wondering how I know about it, aren't you?' she said. 'In our hospital some of the patients swear I can almost read their minds, so don't be surprised when I can guess what you're thinking. Well, I know the form about Simon Tasker, because he happened to be my boy-friend. I met him long before Vicky did. I introduced them, in fact. But Miss Tollard had to prove her universal charm as usual, and for a while he left me. Then you came

185

on the scene. And the rest you can probably imagine for yourself – our affair started again . . . But what you're certainly not aware of is this: Simon Tasker came back from Venice last Tuesday. On Wednesday evening Vicky went round to his flat in Kinnerton Street. I know because I met her leaving it. I can give you the exact time. It was ten minutes to eight. And it was that evening they'd made their plans to spend this week-end together. And I know that's the truth because Simon told me. It came out when he tried to break it to me gently that it was all over between the two of us.'

Muriel turned away from him and walked over to the piano. Her finger moved along the lid as if searching for dust.

'My life's been messed up by Vicky, and I don't want yours to be,' she said.

Graham felt the blood pulsing in the nape of his neck. Muriel gave a short, almost triumphant laugh. 'You still don't believe me,' she said. 'I suppose there's no reason why you should. But there's one easy way to prove it to yourself. Telephone to Larkin.' She laughed again as she moved from the piano. 'Shall I do it for you?' she asked, crossing to the telephone.

He stood up and took the receiver from her hand. 'I don't need to check up on Vicky,' he said. He replaced the receiver on the cradle.

'If you want to bury your head in the sand, you can,' Muriel said quietly. 'Not that I blame you.' She was so close to him that he caught the smell of the scent that Vicky used. 'You know, Graham – I hope you don't mind me calling you "Graham", but it would seem stupid not to now, wouldn't it? I wish we'd got to know each other better from the start. I could have told you from the very first evening you came round to the flat that you didn't stand a chance.'

He could sense an animal warmth coming from her, and he longed to move away. His dislike of her was stifling him, but he forced a smile. 'A chance of what?' he asked, measuring out his politeness stiffly with each word.

'A chance of any success with Vicky. How many years older than her are you? Twenty-six? Twenty-seven? It doesn't really matter. If you'd only been ten years older than Vicky you'd still have been sunk because she only likes boys of her own age. After all, I've been round the town with her. I ought to know.'

She straightened her body so that her breasts pressed against the silk of her blouse. In a daze of misery and disgust Graham listened to the cultivated voice as it continued assiduously.

'You're quite attractive, I don't mind telling you. And I dare say lots of girls run after you, and I don't blame them. You've got quite good looks and you've kept your figure *and* your hair, which is just as important to a man as to a woman, I always say. But you never had a hope with Vicky because she's got a thing about not going to bed with anyone older than herself. Mind you, I think that's a lot of nonsense. After all, it's charm and vitality that count, and they're not dependent on age. You learn *that*, working in a hospital, as you learn a great many other facts about life.'

Her arms swung a little behind her as she spoke and she raised her head towards him.

'I find it perfectly natural that a man of let's say forty-five should want to have an affair with a girl of twenty,' she said. 'But he must choose the right girl.'

Muriel smoothed down her close-fitting skirt and watched her slender reflection in the looking-glass above the drink-tray.

'The girl's got to have a good body and she has to be

passionate,' she said. 'That goes without saying. She's got to be slim and she must have experience. After all, technique counts, doesn't it? But the girl's got to be a companion to the man as well as a lover, especially if he's a person of some distinction in the world. And Vicky could never make a satisfactory companion – she's far too selfish.'

Muriel turned from the looking-glass and stared straight at Graham. He saw the corners of her mouth tremble and her lips part. He fixed his glance at the Guillaumin painting, aware that at any moment her body might touch his.

'You must face the truth of it, Graham,' she said quietly. 'You've chosen the wrong girl this time.'

Graham was determined not to meet her gaze, but as if drawn by some hypnotic force he found his eyes moving inexorably towards her. And desperately he exerted his willpower to avoid looking at her because he did not wish to be needlessly cruel. He knew that though he could control his voice sufficiently to muffle such tones of dislike as it might reveal, and though he could subdue any gesture of hostility that his hands might make, he could do nothing to disguise the expression in his eyes – nothing to conceal the message she would read there of hatred and blatant contempt. But his gaze had passed the sofa now and unless he made a yet stronger effort he would look at her. And even as he exerted himself in pity for her, their eyes met for an instant.

In silence Muriel turned away from him and walked out of the room.

Graham took up the telephone with its long white flex and sat down on the sofa and rang directory inquiries. There was, 'after all', as the wretched girl had kept saying, a very small chance that Muriel had been lying.

188

'Directory inquiries here.'

'The name is Tollard,' he said. 'T.O.L.L.A.R.D. and the house is called Larkin – L.A.R.K.I.N. – and it's in south-west Wiltshire. I think that's enough for you to locate it . . . Yes, thank you . . . And my number . . .'

He waited in a haze of misery. He so dreaded the moment when Muriel's accusation could be confirmed that he was dismayed at the promptness with which he was given the number. 'Plowden 347.' Plowden was obviously the name of the local village. He took a sip of his drink and asked for the number. Cradling the receiver under his chin he lit a cigarette. He could hear the number ringing.

'Plowden three four seven.' It was a pleasant voice that had answered the telephone – a voice that belonged to an educated woman of middle age. It might well be Vicky's mother. Graham could feel his heart pounding against his shirt.

'Could I speak to Miss Vicky Tollard?' Graham asked.

'Victoria's up in town,' the pleasant voice said. 'If you like to hold on a minute I can give you her address.'

'Thanks so much.'

'Here it is,' the voice said. 'Have you got a piece of paper and a pencil to write it down?'

'Yes,' he said, 'I have.' But he made no effort to stretch out for the pad lying by the telephone, for he knew the address he would be given, and he was right. It was the old address in Earl's Court.

'Thank you very much.'

'Not at all,' the friendly voice said. 'Good-bye.'

4

He had left the living-room door open, so that he could hear the sound of the key turning in the latch. Vicky put down her suitcase in the hall and hurried into the room. A wisp of hair had fallen over her left eye and she brushed it back and smiled at him. She was out of breath and he could see her breasts rising and falling.

'Hello!' she cried as she walked in. 'Sorry I'm late as usual. But it really wasn't my fault. There wasn't a seat on the whole train – except in the first class. I had to stand in the corridor. And the wretched train didn't even arrive at the station on time. And you know what buses are like at this hour.'

Graham turned slowly to face her. 'How are things at Larkin?' he asked.

As he spoke Vicky stopped moving towards him. She stood motionless watching him. Then as she saw his expression her face stiffened and she took a deep breath.

'I'd be grateful if you could hurry,' he said. 'We're due at the Benons' dinner-party in ten minutes' time.'

For an instant she remained by the sofa, tense and staring at him. Then she released her breath in a long sigh and swung round towards the door and left the room.

They drove down Park Lane in silence. Suddenly Graham remembered the first evening they had driven alone together in the Bentley – when he had taken her back to her flat and they had stayed talking in front of the shabby columns. 'If you're really prepared to be satisfied with the little I've got to offer you,' she had said, 'then so far as I'm concerned – I'd love us to meet again. And let's see how it all pans out.' Well, it had panned out in deceit, and he was now only conscious of a fierce desire to hurt her.

'What was the hotel like?' he asked. 'I mean the hotel you both spent the week-end at – six miles north of Oxford.'

Vicky was silent. He could feel his hands trembling as he held the wheel. He was close to losing control, and an important evening lay ahead. In order to clear Vicky from his mind for an instant, he tried to think about George and Edna Benon. Graham smiled grimly to himself.

George was a Syrian who had entered the film world before the war as a chartered accountant. In those extravagant and disorderly days when companies were formed over a gin at Quaglino's and went bankrupt three months later over a whisky-sour at the Carlton, chartered accountants were tolerated as part of the process of evolution, but were of less importance than actresses or script-writers. But with post-war austerity and the new Government subsidies, the position changed. Officials in charge of Government organizations such as the National Film Finance Corporation were unwilling to go to a champagne-breakfast-party with a couple of Hungarians on a houseboat at Henley in order to launch a new film company. They required a sober presentation at their office of assets, budgets and all relevant facts, from the cost of hiring the studio to the box-office returns of the producer's previous films. And since many of the most successful pre-war film-makers were unable to understand even the simplest balance sheet and would never contemplate composing one, the chartered accountants crept into positions of importance throughout the industry. And gradually, inspired by the simple vanity that makes most men secretly convinced they could succeed at their neighbour's profession, they began to believe they could make films as well as prepare the budgets for them. And by then a few of them had gained such power that no one could stop them. Such a person was George Benon, and he had displayed an unusual flair for knowing what the lowest common denominator in public taste required in musicals or horror-comics. George was a success. His only mistake – so they said in Wardour Street – had been to marry Edna. He had met her in 1936 when she was a doe-eyed starlet, kept her for a year, and married her when an assistant cameraman had proposed to her.

Edna Benon was now squat and middle-aged. She was grotesquely fat with a mottled face and dyed red hair. Dieticians had failed to reduce her weight, psychotherapists and hypnotists had failed to reduce her daily intake of alcohol, and the combined efforts of George's friends had failed to reduce her influence over him. She must, Graham decided, possess virtues he had not discovered.

They were approaching Chester Square. The Benons' house was re-designed throughout once every five years. But whether the style was Empire or ultra-modern, Graham noticed that small Levantine touches in the shape of pouffes or Damascene rugs crept in, and this pleased him, for it lent a homely touch to the expensive bleak perfection wrought by the furnishing department of some fashionable store. Graham turned to Vicky who was staring at the road ahead. Her face somehow looked smaller and narrower than usual – and younger, too. And her expression was so forlorn that, as he stopped the car in front of the Benons' house, for an instant he longed to take her in his arms. But immediately he remembered her deceit. His voice was sharp as he spoke.

'Make an effort to behave this evening, will you?' he said. 'I know it's not important to you, but it is to me.'

She nodded her head. He opened the car door for her, and together they walked up the steps of the house.

George's hands were spread out like a conjuror as he demanded silence from the group round him for the end of his after-dinner story. 'So Isidore gets himself a telephone installed at the back of *his* car,' George continued. 'And the first thing he does is he rings up Abie's Cadillac. "Abie," he says, "I'm speaking to you from my Rolls and I'm riding down Fifth Avenue." "Excuse me," Abie says, "I can't speak to you just now. I'm busy on the other line."'

Graham joined politely in the laughter. Jewish stories distressed him, particularly when they were stale and unfunny. He wondered if George from Beirut realized that Arabs and Jews were equally Semitic. He glanced blearily across the drawing-room which was at present early eighteenth-century. He had drunk too much throughout the evening in an attempt to bolster his morale, and he was feeling sick and exhausted. Vicky, looking very slender in her new dress, was talking to Carl Dwight and appearing to relish each instant of their conversation. Carl Dwight was a thin, narrow-lipped man who owned three London theatres but was mainly interested in race-horses and the English aristocracy. He was at his happiest during Ascot week when he could combine the two. He fancied himself as a raconteur, and Vicky was now listening with devout interest to a story he was telling her. She had not spoken to Graham all evening, but their eyes had met once in cold hostility across the table.

'You're not on form this evening, Graham.'

He turned to find Edna Benon beside him with a large glass of whisky in her hand.

'You didn't make one single crack at dinner,' she said. 'What's wrong with you? I expect my favourite film director to sparkle at my parties. Wasn't the company to your liking?'

'It's been a wonderful evening, Edna,' he said. 'And I've enjoyed every moment despite a cracking headache.'

She made no reply but peered up at him through her blood-shot eyes. Her mottled red face clashed with her carrot-coloured hair. She looked like a worn rubber doll.

'I'm glad you've fixed up a meeting with George next week,' she said. 'He's quite interested in your Abdel Krim project. He's told me already.'

'I'm glad,' Graham said, searching round for an ashtray for his cigarette.

Edna took a long drink from her glass. 'I find your girl-friend's quite pretty in an off-beat kind of way,' she said. 'But I must confess I can't admire her manners.'

'I'm sorry to hear that,' Graham said. As he spoke, his eyes fell on a small glass dish embedded in an ebony-and-mother-of-pearl surround that stood on a Sheraton side-table. The Levant had mercifully crept in once again in the guise of an ashtray. He leaned across and put out his cigarette. 'What happened?' he asked.

'Well, while you men were chatting over your port and cigars downstairs, we women up here started talking about Morocco – arising out of your Abdel Krim story, which I must say you told well, though perhaps not quite as well as I've heard you tell a story before. Anyhow, I happened to say that I'd love to live in Morocco if it wasn't for the Moroccans, and your young friend – what's her name? Vicky something-or-other? – jumped right down my throat. She as good as called me race-conscious – that was a fine one, me being married to a Syrian – and I was called a snob. I've never known such rudeness. And in my own drawing-room, what's more.'

'I'm sorry, Edna,' Graham said. 'I know that Vicky's been rather overwrought these last few weeks . . .' Then he stopped, for Vicky was approaching them.

'Graham, I'm feeling very tired,' she said. 'Do you mind if we go home?'

'Do you have to drag Graham away from us?' Edna demanded. 'Can't we ring for a taxi to take you home? Or aren't you allowed out alone at night?'

'It's all right, Vicky,' Graham said rapidly. Then he turned back to Edna, who was glowering up at Vicky over her glass. 'Please forgive us,' he said. 'I'm sorry I didn't sparkle, but I have got a ghastly headache, and I have to fly to Paris at crack of dawn.'

'You're breaking up the party,' Edna said truculently. 'You realize that?'

'No, we're not, Edna,' Graham said, looking over her shoulder. 'Here are Carl and Helen Dwight coming to take their leave of you.'

Edna wheeled round to face the advancing couple.

'You're not going too, are you?' she asked.

'I'm afraid we must,' Carl Dwight said firmly. 'I have a rehearsal tomorrow morning.' Then he turned to Graham. 'Your charming young friend has accepted an invitation for you both to a party at our house Wednesday week. I hope that fits in with your plans?'

'Fine,' Graham murmured. 'Thanks . . . fine.'

The Dwights made their farewells to Edna and moved

away, and as Edna switched her attention back to Graham, Vicky spoke to her.

'I hope you'll be coming to their party too,' she said in a tone of aloof politeness.

Edna focused her gaze on Vicky and eyed her in silence for an instant, lowering her head and shuffling her feet on the carpet as if she were in an arena. Then she hurled out her words in a livid attack.

'I may tell you that I happen to have been the *first* person to be invited to their party,' she said. 'In fact it's practically being given in my honour. I may also point out that you met Carl and Helen Dwight for the very first time this evening. But they happen to have been intimate friends of mine for over twenty years.'

Vicky glanced in outraged astonishment at her hostess.

'Good night,' Vicky said and walked briskly towards the door.

'You'd better go with her, Graham,' Edna said. She was shaking with anger, and beads of foam had clustered at the corner of her mouth.

His legs suddenly felt weak, and he leaned against the back of the sofa for support while his words continued unchecked, forming sentence after sentence, filling the room with their sound, pouring out effortlessly, flooding into the silence, spurting out under full pressure, as if his voice had no connection with his trembling body.

'And I can see your future so clearly,' he said, 'because it's the future of every thoroughly spoilt and selfish person. Your features will have coarsened, your body will have lost its slenderness, your skin its smoothness, and that youthful innocent charm will have gone. But you won't have realized any of that – because you're far too conceited and deceitful. And deceitful people often end up by deceiving themselves. So you won't know that your attractive qualities have decayed and gone, and you'll still be equally demanding and equally capricious. And to get what you want from life you'll have to concede more and more. You'll have to make deeper sacrifices. You'll have to lower your standards each year – until you end up a raddled, spoilt, middle-aged, embittered woman without a single friend even in the third-rate world you inhabit.'

Graham gazed down at Vicky who was sitting, expressionless, in the arm-chair near the piano.

'The trouble is that you're fundamentally mean,' he said. 'You're so mean that you're prepared to travel third class to save a few shillings, though it means having to sit on your suitcase for two hours, rather than pay a little more and travel in comfort. It's not that you can't afford it.

I asked you particularly to get back in time for the Benons' dinner-party. But would you fish in that little purse of yours and take a taxi? No. Vicky Tollard is saving up for a car, so let a whole dinner-party wait. . . . You see, it's an all-embracing meanness. You're incapable of giving anything to anyone. You just grab everything you can get out of life, and your arrogance is such that you feel it's all your due.'

He crossed to the drink-tray and poured the rest of the whisky-bottle into his glass.

'Why did you have to offend Edna Benon tonight?' he asked. 'You realize that George Benon is important to me, and yet you went out of your way to alienate his wife. And why did you? I'll tell you exactly why . . . You know, Vicky, one of the advantages of reaching the advanced age of forty-five – which seems so very old to you – one of the advantages is that you learn about people. And I've met your type once before in my life. Only once. But I can recognize it now. And that's how I *know* why you tried to bitch me with the Benons this evening. It was because subconsciously you always want to bring me down to your own level. Subconsciously you resent my success. You dislike such little fame as I may have achieved. You're jealous of such talent as I've got. Subconsciously you want me to fail as a person and to fail in my profession.'

Graham put down his glass and strode across to her armchair and stood over her, glaring down at her as she sat hunched up and rigid. The corner of her mouth was quivering.

'I'll tell you the form, Vicky,' he said. 'I'll tell you what makes you tick. You see, I've found out during the long months I've known you. I've discovered your secret. You're a destroyer, Vicky, and you always have been. Even as a child you were a destroyer. You loved your panda, didn't you? But you destroyed him. And what about young Hamido in Tangier? He was quite happy till you came along and decided it would be amusing to make him fall in love with you. And as usual you succeeded, didn't you? Just as you succeeded with Simon Tasker so as to get him away from Muriel. But Simon Tasker's hard and sophisticated. Hamido isn't – he took it all seriously. He told his friend Ibrahim he was in love with you. He even wanted to take you to meet his mother in Fez. Do you know what that means? And if you do know, does it even disturb you for a single second? I doubt it. Hamido's destroyed now. He's as burnt up as the panda in your nursery grate. He's finished.'

Graham bent forward and rapped the side of the armchair with the back of his hand.

'But *I'm* not finished,' he cried. 'Far from it. You've tried your best to destroy me. You've undermined my self-confidence. You've made me lose all peace of mind. But you haven't destroyed me – though God knows you've tried hard enough. You haven't destroyed me yet, and I'm not going to give you another chance.'

Suddenly Vicky broke into tears. She began to sob unrestrainedly, like a child. Tears coursed down her cheeks, halted for a moment on her lips and then ran down her chin, while her hand fumbled at her underlip. And as Graham looked at her small body shaken with the passion of her grief, through the mist of his drunkenness he became aware that the voice that had pounded against the walls of the room belonged to him and was his responsibility. She was choking with her sobs, and he knew, now, that he had caused them. He leaned over and put his arms round her and tried to draw her close to him.

'Don't touch me,' she said with a shudder. 'Don't touch me.'

Then it seemed to him that yet once again a gesture he had made had been rejected, and an overture of love had been ignored. He drew away from her as if she were contaminated.

'All right,' he said. 'Play it your own way.'

He stood over the drink-tray, trying to decide what to take now the whisky was finished. Vaguely he was aware that Vicky had risen from the arm-chair and had gone out through the door. He reached out for the bottle of brandy, and the label seemed to move. He could hear her footsteps moving down the passage towards her own room, and he took his glass and sat down on the sofa.

'Don't touch me.' It was yet another refusal, another defeat. And as her voice rang like a clarion in his ears, his mind swung back to their bedroom in Tangier . . .

He could even smell the saline odour from the bathroom mingled with the jasmine on the wall outside. The night was warm, and they had not pulled down the heavy shutters. She lay naked on the wide bed beside him. He rolled over so that their bodies were almost touching. He began to stroke her shoulder, then slid his hand down to her breasts.

'I love you,' he said. 'Do you know that?'

Vicky was silent. Graham could see all the slenderness of her body in the light of the moon over the roof-tops. His hand slipped over the soft skin of her stomach and came to rest between her thighs. They had quarrelled earlier that evening, but now he was only conscious of a profound peace such as a traveller might feel who has journeyed across a barren desert and has at last reached green palm trees and security. But suddenly Vicky moved abruptly away from him and shifted to the far side of the bed.

'Don't touch me, Graham,' she said. 'Do you mind? It's far too hot for sex tonight, and you simply radiate heat.'

And he had turned his head away from her and had lain staring at the moonlight, thinking of one of the other girls he might have brought out with him to Tangier and who might now be lying naked beside him . . .

He was disturbed by a loud tinkle which came from the receiver by the sofa. The extension of the telephone was being used. Graham was tempted to pick up the receiver and listen. It was only middle-class training, he thought as he drank his whisky, that prevented him from listening to Vicky's conversation. Presently there was a click as Vicky's door opened and he heard her footsteps going along the passage. He stumbled across the living-room and out into the hall, resting his weight heavily against the lintel of the door. He felt the glass in his hand begin to slip, and he watched it slide slowly through his fingers until he held only the rim and it fell noiselessly on to the carpet. He saw that Vicky was moving towards the front door of the flat, carrying a small suitcase. He stood looking at her dazedly. Through the fog of alcohol he knew that for some reason he was unwilling to speak. He watched her draw closer to the door. He realized that she was about to leave him, but at that instant the fact seemed unimportant. He felt detached from the scene as if he were watching it on a small screen from far back in the stalls. Her hand rose towards the handle of the door, and at that instant he woke from his dream. The fog lifted, and reality pierced his mind like a shaft of sunlight. If Vicky left now he would be alone tomorrow – and the next day, and perhaps for ever.

'Stop,' he said.

He moved unsteadily towards her, his arms outstretched. But as he advanced, without looking at him Vicky opened the door swiftly and closed it behind her, and he heard the sound of the mortice lock turning in the latch from the other side. He tried to wrench open the door, though he knew the effort was futile. He searched in his pockets for his keys but could not find them. He heard the lift-door close and the whine of the lift descending. He glanced at the hall-table, then rushed into the living-room. He could not remember where he had put his keys on their return from the Benons' party. He lurched round the room, searching frantically, peering at the flat surface of tables and chairs and of the piano. Then he heard a taxi draw up in the street below. He hurried across the room and pulled aside the heavy curtains and looked down. In the harsh light of the street lamp he saw Vicky get into the taxi with the small shabby suitcase in her hand. He flung open the window and leaned out. To his dismay he realized that the taxi had begun to move.

'Vicky!' he called wildly.

The taxi-driver glanced up briefly through his side window, and for an instant Graham thought that he would stop, but the taxi slowly gathered speed and drove along the street and then turned left and disappeared. Graham remained for a while gripping the window-ledge and leaning out as if his fingers were fastened to the ledge. Then he closed the window and drew the curtains. As he turned back into the living-room he saw his bunch of keys lying on the carpet by the sofa. He wandered into the hall and unlocked the front door and opened it and gazed out hopelessly at the polished wooden panelling on either side of the lift. He went back into the flat. He closed the door behind him, and walked along the passage to Vicky's bedroom. He pushed open the bedroom door. He still clung to a confused hope that her departure was not final. He peered into the room. The sliding door of the wardrobe which stretched the length of the far wall was open. He was reassured to see her clothes on the coat-hangers. Then his eyes drifted to the bed and stopped. He felt his body lurch forward and for a moment he thought he would fall. Lying on the bed were the two gold bracelets he had given her in Tangier.

Slowly Graham shambled back to his bedroom. He took three sleeping pills and began to undress.

6

His head was throbbing, and Cole was standing beside his bed, talking to him.

'Wake up, Graham,' Cole was saying. 'You must wake up or you'll miss your plane.'

Consciousness seeped back, and the recollection of the previous night swept over him. He shuddered with the pain. His mouth was so dry that he could not speak. He stretched out for the tumbler of water on the bed-side table. Cole noticed his shaking hand and smiled.

'Whatever did you get up to last night?' he asked. 'Mrs Lucas has been knocking on your door for ages.'

Graham finished the glass of water and looked at his watch. It was five past eight.

'Last night,' he said, 'or it may have been in the early hours of this morning – I simply don't know – I had the most ghastly row with Vicky . . . I can't remember all I said, but it must have been horrible and bloody. And Vicky walked out of the flat.'

He took the cigarette Cole offered him.

'Now listen, Cole. I want you to help me. Vicky probably won't speak to me, so will you telephone her for me? The last thing I want to do is to involve you in my troubles, but she'll speak to you, I'm sure. Either she'll have gone back to the old flat she shared with Muriel Craig – which I doubt – or she'll be at Simon Tasker's flat in Kinnerton Street. You'll find both numbers in the blue book by the phone in the living-room. Could you be terribly kind and try to find her. And if you speak to her, could you say tha

I'm desperately sorry. If you could possibly persuade her to speak to me, that would be wonderful. But at least tell her how wretched I feel about it all.'

'Sure,' Cole said and left the room.

Mrs Lucas always laid out the morning mail neatly on the hall-table. In a daze of sickness, Graham put on a dressing-gown and walked along the passage to the hall. Picking up a stack of envelopes, he noticed a parcel lying at the far end of the table. He glanced quickly through his letters. None had been sent by hand. Lying beside the parcel was a letter addressed to Miss Victoria Tollard. He stared down at it dully. The pain in his head was making him feel giddy. Vaguely he registered the fact that one of the telephones was ringing, but the sound was so distant that it might have come from another flat. He took up the envelope and hesitated. The paper was expensive, and the writing was firm and even. He ripped open the envelope. Inside was a sheet of stiff paper. It was a receipt from Cartier, made out in the name of Miss Victoria Tollard, for a pair of ivory hair-brushes with gold monograms. Cole had appeared in the hall and was standing beside him and he handed him the receipt. He looked at the parcel which was about eighteen inches long and a foot deep and had been sent by registered post. Inside were two ivory-backed hair-brushes. He took out one of them and examined it. Inlaid into the curved back of the white ivory were the letters G and H skilfully entwined – his monogram.

'So *that's* what she was really saving up for all this time,' Cole said.

Graham covered his eyes with his hands. Cole touched his shoulder.

'Graham,' he said, 'it's Edna Benon on the phone for you.'

'Tell her I'm in conference and can't speak to her.'

'I've done that. But she says it's urgent.'

'Have you tried those two numbers?'

'I have. Simon Tasker's doesn't answer, and the other one's engaged. Graham, you *must* talk to Edna.'

'Right.'

'She's on your ex-directory line – needless to say.'

Graham walked into his bedroom and took up the green receiver.

'Graham here,' he said.

'Oh, thank heavens I got you,' Edna's voice crackled in his ear. 'I've been lying awake all night worrying. I really feel quite ill from the strain of it all. You see, I simply *had* to get hold of you to apologize. I'm so terribly sorry about last night. I'm afraid I was a bit high. And I may tell you that George is positively black with rage at me. I really am most profoundly sorry. And please will you give my abject apologies to that charming young girl who was with you?'

'Let's forget about it.'

'Can I tell George that all's well between us and your conference next week is still on?'

'You can.'

'Bless you, Graham. You'll always be my favourite, *favourite* director. You do know that.'

'See you when I get back from Paris,' Graham said.

As he put down the receiver, Cole came into the bedroom. 'I've got on to Vicky's old flat,' Cole said. 'Muriel Craig wasn't there. It seems she's away on holiday. But there was a girl-friend of hers staying there – a nurse at the hospital. And the nurse said that she'd been in all evening and all night and Vicky hadn't phoned once. And I'm pretty sure she was telling the truth.'

'Then Vicky must be at Simon Tasker's flat.'

'His phone doesn't answer, and if you don't leave this instant, Graham, you're going to miss that plane.'

'I'll catch the next one.'

'And miss the conference?'

'To hell with the conference.'

'No, Graham,' Cole said firmly. 'You're going to catch the plane and you're going to attend the conference. You're not the only person involved, remember? Mrs Lucas has packed your bag. I'll contact Vicky if I can and I'll phone you at the hotel this evening in any event. Okay? So now get cracking.'

7

WHILE he waited in his sitting-room for his personal call to London, Graham went through the notes he had taken during the conference. For over three hours he had struggled in an ill-ventilated, long, narrow room flanked by busts of nineteenth-century French composers who all looked remarkably alike – perhaps because they wore their hair in the same flowing style. He had been in turn firm, persuasive, modestly charming and arrogant. He had been fluent and he had exuded confidence. But he knew quite well that his victory was due to the enthusiastic reviews of *The Strawberry Patch* in the French Press. The film was now running in two cinemas in Paris and playing to capacity at both. Graham had become a celebrity overnight, and the backers realized it. Graham now had the money to make Abdel Krim into what the industry called 'a major picture'.

The telephone rang and he lifted the receiver, knowing that Simon Tasker was at the other end of the line.

'Graham Hadley here,' he said. 'I'm calling you from Paris because I'm terribly worried about Vicky. Is she with you?'

'No,' Simon Tasker said. 'She's not with me now.' His voice was cautious but not hostile.

'But you've seen her?'

'Yes, I have. She came round to my flat at about three this morning. I'm afraid she was awfully upset. In fact, she was quite hysterical.'

'So she's staying with you?'

'No,' Simon said. 'She stayed what remained of last night, of course. But she insisted on leaving this morning, though I tried to persuade her not to. She's moved into an hotel.'

'Do you know *what* hotel?'

There was a pause. 'Yes,' Simon said reluctantly. 'I do know, but Vicky made me promise not to tell you.'

Graham swallowed. 'I see,' he said. 'So I suppose that even if I tell you that I'm desperate to get in touch with her you won't tell me the name?'

'I'm afraid not.'

'You can't even let me have some hint?'

'Sorry.' The voice was very definite.

'Could I write to her at your flat?'

'You could,' Simon said. 'But she asked me to give you a message. I was to tell you not to bother to write to her because she'd burn the letter before reading it. Like she burnt her panda, I was to tell you.'

Graham kept his voice calm. 'Will you be seeing her?'

'I expect so. In fact, she may be dining with me tonight.'

'Can you give her a message from me?'

'Certainly.'

'Can you please tell her that I'm deeply sorry about last night. And say that I'm thrilled with the present – she'll know what I mean. And tell her . . .' Graham checked himself. He had been about to ask Simon to deliver a more intimate message. He made an effort to recover his usual poise. 'Tell her I've been positively dripping sack-cloth and ashes all over the film conference,' he said.

'Right. I'll tell her that.'

'I'm most grateful to you,' Graham said, and was about to put down the receiver when the young man spoke again.

'Mr Hadley . . .'

'Yes?'

'When are you coming back to London?'

'Sunday morning.'

'Could we meet?'

'I don't see why not.' Graham's slight hesitation could not have been noticed. 'Can you come round to my flat on Sunday evening at six o'clock?'

'That'll do fine,' Simon said. 'And I'll pass on your messages.'

'Thanks,' Graham said. 'Goodbye.'

8

SIMON TASKER picked up the Adam-and-Eve box and turned it over in his large hands.

'Splendid workmanship,' he said. 'Regency, of course.'

Simon had gained confidence, Graham noticed, since his success in Larry's film (apparently the rushes had been excellent) and he was better dressed. Simon put down the box on the table and turned to face Graham.

'Can I tell you the reason I wanted to meet you as soon as you got back?' he asked. 'I hope you won't be annoyed with me?'

'Go ahead and we'll see.'

'I want to know, if I may, just what you said to Vicky that last night.'

Graham stared at him. 'Why do you?'

Simon picked up his drink and began shaking it gently so that the ice tinkled against the side of the glass.

'You know all about that week-end we spent near Oxford,' Simon said. 'In fact, I gather that was half the reason for your row. Well, during the week-end I got the impression that my relationship with Vicky was to be resumed – to put it quite bluntly, though I realized that you must always come first. In fact, she made it pretty clear that's what the form was. But I felt that at least I'd come on the scene once again.'

He put down his glass and looked across at Graham.

'But I obviously hadn't,' he said.

'Why?'

'Well, I've tried to puzzle it out, and the only explanation I can think of is that you said something to her that put her against me for good.'

'And are you so naïve that you can believe that if I *had* said something of that kind I'd tell you what it was?'

Simon uncrossed his legs and stretched them.

'I was afraid you'd be annoyed,' he said.

'I'm not annoyed. I'm just amazed at your trust in human nature generally, and in me in particular.'

Simon smiled at him. That smile, Graham thought, might make him a star if he could act at all adequately.

'*Did* you say something to her?' Simon asked.

Graham grinned. There was a quality of directness about Simon that was rather appealing, and he could understand what Vicky found attractive about him.

'I can't remember all I said that night,' Graham replied. 'But I promise you that I can't recollect anything I can have said to put her against you . . . And now may I ask you a question?'

'Please do.'

'You gave Vicky my message?'

'Yes.'

'What did she say?'

'She was still pretty incoherent. But she said you'd called her a destroyer, and she said there was one person she wasn't going to destroy.'

'And that person was presumably herself.'

'I don't know. I couldn't make it out.'

'Second question,' Graham said. 'Where is she now?'

'At Larkin.'

'How do you know?'

'I went round to her hotel an hour or so after I'd

212

spoken to her on the phone, because she'd half promised to have dinner with me. She was more controlled but still rather odd. She couldn't dine with me, she said, because she was going down to Wiltshire by train. I drove her to the station and she promised to call me. But she hasn't phoned once.'

After Simon had left the flat, Graham rang Cole.

'At least you now know where she is,' Cole said after he had listened to Graham's report. 'That's one consolation. What will you do next? Have you tried phoning Larkin?'

'I'm afraid to do that,' Graham said. 'I know instinctively that if I phone her or send a telegram she'll know I'm on my way there and she'll leave. My only hope now is to drive down to Larkin early tomorrow morning and walk straight in.'

'Then promise me one thing, Graham.'

'What's that?'

'Promise me that however things go at Larkin you'll drive back to London, with or without Vicky, and dine with me at the Hermitage tomorrow night to celebrate the enduring solid fact that we're launched on Abdel Krim in a big way.'

'I promise.'

'Your mind's far away again. I can tell from your voice. *Now* what are you thinking about?'

'I was just thinking that all my accusations against Vicky could be turned against me,' Graham said. 'It may be that *I'm* the destroyer. Vicky was quite happy before I appeared on the horizon. I've hardly contributed to her contentment, have I?'

213

'Nor she to yours,' Cole said. 'But that's not the point, as I once tried to tell you. There may be darkness and rats in the Garden of Eden. But it's Eden just the same – for those that can take it.'

9

On the way down to Wiltshire, driving in warm September sunshine, Graham managed to keep himself from thinking constantly about Vicky by selecting the whole cast for Abdel Krim from living actors irrespective of their availability or cost. But when he approached the outskirts of Plowden, Vicky crept back into his mind, and, for some reason, he began to think about her contact lenses. He could see her putting them one by one into her mouth to clean them.

'Surely that's not what the makers intended,' Graham had said laughing the first time he had seen the operation.

'There's a special liquid for cleaning them, but it's wildly expensive, and anyhow I've lost it,' Vicky had replied.

Once, while talking to him in the bathroom she had popped a lens into her mouth to clean it and suddenly a look of astonishment had crossed her face followed by an expression of horror.

'I've swallowed it,' she had said. And without hesitating she had knelt down on the tiled floor and stuck a finger down her throat and had retched until she brought it up.

Vicky had three different types of lenses: untinted for everyday use, when her eyes remained their natural grey-green colour, blue for glamour, and brown for bright sunshine. He found the change from a Scandinavian ice-blue gaze to Neapolitan dark-brown stare disconcerting, and he had never grown used to the sight of a lens when it had slipped in her eye. On the Atlantic beach in Tangier, he

215

remembered, she had loved riding inshore on the long rolling breakers. He had been lying in the sun when suddenly she had waded back into the shallows and called out for him.

'Can you see it?' she asked when he had joined her. 'It's slipped.' She raised her head and pulled up her right eyelid with her fingers. 'Can't you see it?'

'No.'

'It's not in the far corner?'

'No.'

She began to prod her lids with her little finger.

'It must have slipped under the top lid,' she said. 'Wait a moment . . . No, it won't work. We'll have to get on dry land, or if it drops out I'll lose it.'

On the sand, she groped into her eye with her first and second fingers, and a tiny dark brown circle appeared from below her lid.

'*Now* can you see it?'

'Yes. It's dead centre just above your iris . . . Here.' And he pointed to the position on his own eye. Vicky pulled back the lid and tried to manœuvre it downwards, but it slid into the corner.

'*Now* where is it?'

Her moist, glazed eye reminded him of a fish he had once caught as a child when his father had insisted on taking him on an angling expedition, and watching the lens slide across her eye had made him feel slightly sick. He had been thankful when it had slipped back into position again.

Why, Graham wondered as he turned the Bentley down the turning to the right that was marked 'Plowden', why had he thought of incidents connected with her lenses? Why had he not remembered occasions when they had made love together with such passion that the whole world seemed to be comprised only of their two bodies? Why had his mind not dwelled on moments when he had looked

216

down at her lying naked beneath the gilt dragon and had known from her expression as she glanced up at him and by an unconscious movement of her wrist that he had only to lie down beside her and her arms would fold round him and her thighs would slide against him ? Perhaps, he decided hesitantly, perhaps the reason was that her hopelessly poor eyesight was linked in his mind with her incompetence to deal with the problems of everyday life – with her inability to put clothes on hangers or to carry latch-keys. Vicky had aroused his protective instinct more than anyone he had met.

It was eleven o'clock and the pub he was approaching would be open, but Graham passed it. He did not want to meet Vicky's mother reeking of gin. He stopped by the village war memorial and leaned out of the window towards an old man who was reading the sports page of a newspaper.

'Excuse me,' Graham said. 'But could you please tell me the way to Larkin?'

The old man lowered his paper. He was dressed in a faded green suit and his collar was frayed and dirty.

'Larkin,' he said reflectively. 'Ah, Larkin.' His accent might have been local, for there was certainly a burr to it. 'Now for Larkin you should take first right, then take the second turning left up Briar's Lane, then turn right. And then you better ask again,' he concluded firmly.

'Thanks,' Graham said.

'That's a big car you've got there,' the old man said, examining the black Bentley with interest.

Graham was uncertain what to reply. 'It's all right,' he said vaguely.

'I wouldn't have a car like that,' the old man announced. 'Not if you paid me.' And he shuffled off towards the pub.

Graham had followed the directions he had been given and was driving up a narrow lane when he noticed a small boy in a T-shirt and blue shorts crouched on the grass verge about twenty yards ahead of him. As the car approached him, the small boy suddenly darted out from the verge and stood in the middle of the lane and flung out his arms in an attempt to block the road. His arms were outstretched in a gesture that brought back to Graham a hideous memory. The brakes screeched as he pulled up. The small boy scurried round the car to the front offside tyre and stooped down and picked up something.

'Want to get yourself run over ?' Graham asked.

'No,' the boy answered. 'But you've just run over my tortoise.' He held up a flattened odd-shaped piece of metal – which was evidently all that remained of a complicated toy.

Graham felt in his pockets for a coin but could not find one. Without being able to take his eyes from the boy's stricken, hostile face he dived in his breast-pocket and pulled out his wallet. Then he turned away from the boy and looked down. He could not find a ten-shilling note, so he took out a pound note and handed it to the boy.

'This is so you can buy yourself another one,' Graham said.

In silence the boy took the note and stared at it. Then he slowly crumpled it up in his hand, and for a moment Graham thought that he was going to throw it away. But the boy glanced down at the crushed ball of paper and then thrust it deep into the pocket of his shorts.

'Do you know the way to a house called Larkin?' Graham asked.

'It's the second house on the right,' the boy muttered.

'Thanks,' Graham said. 'And I'm sorry about that tortoise.'

But the boy had already turned away.

.   .   .   .   .

After he had passed the first house on the right he saw the grey stone wall – 'high enough to stop people looking over it', Vicky had said when they had played the garden-game at Mae Millington's party, 'but low enough to allow those who really tried'. At the time he had suspected that she had been describing a garden she had known well. The white gate with 'Larkin' written on it was open and he turned and drove through it. A short gravel drive led to a plain grey-stone early-Georgian house with a window on either side of the front door and three windows above it. Graham began to take slow deep breaths as he had done in the war to lessen his fear.

He stopped the car and got out. The sun was shining above the low banks of cloud, and a light breeze was shaking the remaining petals from the rose-bushes that climbed along the wall of the house. His footsteps sounded loud on the gravel as he walked towards the porch. He pulled the brass handle of the bell and waited, watching the petals fall on to the unkempt lawn.

The door was opened by an old woman with untidy white hair and a broad rough-skinned face and chapped red hands. She looked up at Graham inquiringly through steel-rimmed spectacles that had been mended with sealing-wax.

'Good morning,' she said.

Probably, Graham thought, the pleasant-faced woman who was gazing at him placidly was Emmy, the woman who had once been Vicky's nurse and who was now the housekeeper. Then he saw the moles on her cheek and was certain, and this lent him confidence.

'Good morning,' he said. 'I wonder if I can speak to Miss Tollard?'

'She's in the garden,' Emmy said. 'Will you come this way?'

Emmy led him through a high-ceilinged dusty hall paved

in black and white and into an Adam-green drawing-room in which the furniture had obviously been unchanged for the last thirty years. Graham noticed, with a director's eye, the incongruity of the television set on the table in the corner. He would have had it removed. As they crossed the room towards the french windows that opened out on to the garden, Emmy paused.

'What name shall I say?' she asked.

This was a question for which Graham was prepared, for he had realized that if his name was announced to Vicky before he reached her, there was a risk that she would escape or refuse to see him.

'Cole Edwards,' he said.

Graham followed Emmy through the open windows and out into a garden, which was walled on one side and flanked on the other by an untidy herbaceous border marked out with little white stones.

'Lovely day, isn't it?' Emmy said.

'Fine,' Graham agreed. His mouth was dry.

By the brook at the far end of the garden a grey-haired woman of about sixty was sitting in a deck-chair reading a magazine.

'There's Miss Tollard,' Emmy said.

Graham stopped and stood motionless. The woman looked up, rose slowly from her chair, and came towards him. She was tall and thin with a narrow face. Her small head was set on a slender neck from which blue veins protruded. She had faded grey eyes, a high-bridged straight nose, and a broad mouth.

'A Mr Edwards to see you, Miss Jennifer,' Emmy said.

'Good morning,' the woman said, smiling at him uncertainly. It was the same pleasant voice that Graham had heard on the telephone when he rang up Larkin.

'Please forgive me for disturbing you,' Graham said. 'But I was looking for Vicky Tollard.'

'I'm afraid Victoria's not here.'

'You mean she's not in the house?'

'No. She's not.'

'Then I'm sorry,' Graham said, 'but there must be some mistake. I was told Vicky had come down here to stay with her parents.'

The woman smiled rather sadly. Her hands stroked the air in a wavering gesture as if she were tracing some invisible outline.

'Then there certainly must be some mistake,' she said. 'You did say Vicky Tollard, didn't you?'

'Yes.'

'You're a friend of Victoria's?'

'I am.'

The woman's hands rose once again from her side and carved the air apologetically.

'Then I don't understand why you should think she was staying with her parents,' she said.

'That's what I was told.'

'How strange she didn't tell you.'

'Tell me what?'

The woman looked round the garden and gave a little shake of her shoulders as if apologizing to the trees and the walls and the lawn for repeating a story so well known.

'Victoria's parents died thirteen years ago,' she said. 'They were killed in a car accident when she was five years old . . . Her father was my brother . . . This has been Vicky's home ever since.'

As he gaped, staring into the woman's sad grey eyes, Graham's mind switched back and he remembered the night-club to which he had taken Vicky the first evening

221

they had gone out together and he remembered her description of her father. 'In a way,' Graham had said, after he had listened to a detailed report of the grey streaks in his hair and his dark complexion and brown eyes, 'in a way your father sounds a bit like me.' And he could see the look on Vicky's face as she had answered. 'Yes,' she had said. 'I s'pose he is in a way.'

The woman was now watching him with an odd expression. Graham felt that he must say something.

'Hasn't Vicky been down here at all recently?' he asked.

'Strangely enough she came down here almost exactly a week ago, but she only stayed the night, though naturally I tried to persuade her to stay longer.'

Emmy was advancing across the lawn carrying a deck-chair.

'Put it down beside mine, Emmy,' the woman said.

'That's just what I was going to do, Miss Jennifer,' Emmy said quietly.

The woman smiled at her and turned to Graham.

'Shall we sit down, Mr Edwards?' she asked.

'Thanks,' Graham said. 'But I mustn't be long. I promised to turn up for a late lunch with some friends of mine in Salisbury.'

'Well I dare say they'll forgive you if you're a few minutes late,' the woman said, walking towards the chairs by the brook.

'Do you know Vicky well, Mr Edwards?' the woman asked after they had sat down.

'Fairly well.'

'And you're fond of her?' she asked abruptly.

'Very.'

The woman nodded to herself. 'Yes,' she said. 'I can sense that.' For a while she was silent, watching the water swirling over the smooth stones in the brook. 'Of course

'I'm not really surprised that Vicky didn't let you know that her parents were dead,' she said quietly. 'You see, the accident came to her as a terrible shock. In a matter of seconds on a fine autumn afternoon she lost the two people she loved most in the world.'

Her bony fingers twined and untwined relentlessly as she talked.

'Of course, I wasn't living here in those days,' she said. 'But they telephoned to me from the hospital, and I had to come here to break the news to Vicky.'

The woman raised her hands and let them fall back together on her lap.

'She'd always been a highly-strung child, and I was afraid she'd be hysterical. But when I finally broke the truth to her she merely stared at me. I thought she hadn't understood me, so very gently I told her again. But still there were no tears, no sign of emotion. She only stared at me.'

The woman sighed, and for a moment her face reminded him of Vicky.

'At first I believed there must be some streak of callousness in the child's nature that I hadn't understood,' she said. 'But I soon realized I was wrong. You see, the reason that Vicky was so calm when I told her the ghastly news was that she didn't believe it. Some instinct of self-protection – don't they call it "defence-mechanism" nowadays? – refused to allow her to accept the truth.'

The clouds had risen in the sky, and the sun was breaking through them, casting shapeless shadows on the lawn.

'Vicky was an inventive child,' the woman said, 'and by the time the week was out she had convinced herself that her mother and father had gone abroad to India. And she put two photographs that she'd found of them in a little silver photograph-case I'd given her and stood it beside her bed.'

223

A dandelion was growing on the lawn between the deck-chairs, and the woman stooped over and broke it off and tossed it into the stream.

'I was appointed Victoria's guardian,' she said. 'And of course it was a responsibility for me. I asked our doctor whether I should insist on her facing up to the truth and whether I should take her with me to the funeral, and he talked a lot about traumatic shocks and hysterical resistances and I don't know what. However, the upshot of it was that he said that in time Victoria would be strong enough to accept the truth, but in the meantime I must let her continue with the illusion. And so it was.'

The woman's hands moved in a vague, distracted gesture.

'I couldn't tell you the precise moment that she faced the truth. In an odd kind of way I don't think she ever did, and the silver photograph-case never left her bed-side and travelled wherever she went,' the woman continued. 'Victoria had been even more devoted to her father than her mother, and to this day I suspect that she believes he's still with her, probably because she tries to find him in other people. In that sense the illusion still persisted until very recently.'

A nervous tic had started on the right side of her face, and she put up a hand to control it.

'Victoria was a deeply affectionate child,' she said, 'and I think she managed to transfer some of her love to Emmy and some of it to me. Of course I was the wrong kind of person to be her guardian, though I can't think who else they could have chosen. I was devoted to Victoria, and I was far too indulgent. And I'm afraid that as she began to grow up I seemed to lose such little control as I ever had over her. By the time she'd reached seventeen she'd finished school in Switzerland, and I couldn't keep her chained up here at Larkin all twelve months of the year, could I, Mr Edwards? So I let her go up to London to share a flat with a girl she knew well who was working in a hospital, and she found a secretarial job in an advertising office. But I'm afraid she's grown very wild lately.'

The woman glanced up at him.

'You probably knew that she'd given up her job?'

'Yes, I'd heard that.'

'She found some work in films for a while,' the woman said, 'translating some play from the French.'

Her worn grey eyes wandered vaguely across the meadow beyond the brook.

'Since you're a friend of Victoria's,' she said, 'you probably know Mr Hadley.'

'Yes. I do.'

'Victoria met him in May, I think, at some party, and they became great friends. He's far older than she is, as you know. And in a way I think that during these last four months he really did take the place of her father in her life. He helped to continue the illusion. He's got plenty of money, as you probably know, and he gave Vicky the kind of life that the ideal father of her imaginings might have given her. I gathered from the few letters she sent me at the time that she was leading a life filled with huge parties and celebrities and first nights at the theatre.'

Graham was silent. He knew that in time he would find out where Vicky was, and he now dreaded that moment.

'She became quite devoted to him,' the woman said. 'I know *that* not only from her letters but from what she told me when she came down here last Tuesday after their row. Had you heard there had been a row between them?'

'Yes.'

'I'm afraid that Victoria was terribly upset – more upset than I've ever seen her. She'll never see him again, I'm certain. It's the complete end of their friendship. And I'm sure that it was mainly responsible for her decision.'

'What decision?'

The woman glanced at him for an instant, then turned her eyes back to the meadow.

'But of course, Mr Edwards, you don't know,' she said. 'If you'd known you wouldn't have come here, would you? How stupid I'm becoming! Victoria came down here last Tuesday to say good-bye to me for a while and to ask me to sign a document, as one of her trustees, allowing her to withdraw a portion of the money that's coming to her when she's twenty-one. She'd made up her mind to go back to Tangier where she spent her holiday this summer to open a restaurant on the beach for the tourists. She seemed convinced it would make her a fortune. Naturally, I did my best to dissuade her, but once Victoria's made up her mind there's nothing you can do about it. I've never known anyone so obstinate. And, after all, it was only a small portion of what she'll come into when she's twenty-one under the terms of the trust. So in the end I gave in to her.'

The woman looked down at her hands which were now folded peacefully on her lap.

'For some reason Victoria was in a frantic hurry to get to Tangier. It was something to do with a partner she had to find out there. And she left after breakfast on Wednesday morning. She wanted to catch the plane for Morocco that very afternoon. She was in such a hurry that she even left behind the silver case that contained the photographs of her parents, and she has never done that before.'

'Is she in Tangier now?'

'Yes, she is. I had a post-card from her only this morning. I can show it to you, if you like.'

The woman picked up a large bag that was lying beside the chair and rummaged in it.

226

'Here it is,' she said. She took out the post-card and handed it to him. The picture was a brightly-coloured view of the Tangier water-front taken from the beach below Evelyn's bar. Graham turned over the card and recognized Vicky's firm spiky handwriting.

'Wish you were here.
Love,
Vicky.'

As Graham held the card his mind swept back to Tangier and he remembered staring out of the window of their flat. He could feel the close night air and he could see the roof-tops framed by the top of the shutter and the sides of the casement, and he could hear Vicky's drowsy voice as she described the smell that seemed to pervade Morocco. 'It's a sickly smell, and one feels it's centuries old,' she had said. 'It clings to all of them – even the young ones like Hamido. It's a smell of sin. But there's a smell of the earth, and the manger too.' Suddenly he had a vision of Hamido's wide, blunt hands. His head was aching and he felt dazed. He longed to get away from the garden that reminded him of Vicky with every buttercup on the lawn, with every petal of wild-rose on the wall, with every little white stone beside the herbaceous border. He must escape quickly. But there was one question he must ask first.

He turned to the woman and fixed his eyes on her steadily.

'You said that Vicky would never see Graham Hadley again. You said the row between them was a complete end of their friendship. What makes you so sure of that?'

The woman's eyes were sad as they met his gaze.

'Surely the answer to that is simple,' she said gently. 'It's all over between them because when Mr Hadley turned on her so violently he broke the illusion.'

The woman took the post-card from his hand and put it back in her bag.

'I don't know how he did it,' she said. 'But he broke an illusion that she had clung to since she was five years old. And I expect that's why she left her photograph-case behind.'

Suddenly the woman's hands jerked upwards as if pulled by invisible wires.

'You must forgive me,' she cried. 'But I haven't offered you anything to drink. I'm afraid I can only offer you sherry, but if you'd care for a glass . . .'

'Thanks very much,' Graham said, getting up from the deck-chair. 'But I really must be off. I'm terribly late as it is.'

He was wrapped now in a mist of anguish, and his only conscious desire was to get away from the kindly voice which he was vaguely aware was continuing as the woman rose slowly from her chair and stood beside him.

'Of course. Your friends in Salisbury . . . I quite forgot . . . How stupid I'm getting . . .'

'Good-bye, Miss Tollard,' he said with a last desperate attempt to sound controlled. 'Thank you for receiving me. I'm glad to have met you.'

'Good-bye,' she called out as he moved, trembling with haste to escape, across the lawn. 'Good-bye, Mr Hadley.'

It was only when he had reached the french windows and was plunging through the drawing-room towards the hall that he realized she had used his name.

Graham finished the flask of whisky he kept in the locker of his car and drove back along the lane. Moths were fluttering in the hedgerow. The breeze had dropped, and the air was very still. At a slight bend in the lane he saw the small boy. The child was sitting on the grass verge, crouched in the same place and in the same position as he had been when Graham first saw him. In his left hand he was holding the crushed tortoise and gazing down at it. There were smudges beneath his eyes as if he had wiped them with the back of his grimy wrists. The boy saw the Bentley approaching and looked up. As the car passed in front of him, the boy picked up a stone and threw it. The stone struck the heavy coachwork with a thud.

Graham took his foot off the accelerator and hesitated for a moment. He wanted to stop the car because he felt like telling the boy once again that he was sorry he had destroyed his toy. He wanted to apologize for having given the impression that he believed that handing out a pound note could cancel the damage. In his confused misery, Graham now felt guilty for having given the boy false values. He now wanted to explain to him carefully that he recognized that the power of gaining money was not enough. He wanted to tell the boy this so that the boy should not grow up to believe that he in his turn could crush a stranger's possession and be absolved by a cash payment. And perhaps, Graham thought, if he were patient enough – which would mean opening the bottle of whisky in his brief-case – he might even persuade the boy to appreciate the truth of Cole's words which he now dimly perceived, that the failure of mankind was lack of understanding and lack of love and the two were probably the same thing.

But Graham's foot hesitated only for an instant above the brake-pedal before he drove on. For how could he explain to the boy what he himself could still not fully comprehend ? Suddenly he smiled at his sentimentality – an un-needed relic that still remained with him like a lingering smell from the chemist's shop in Birmingham.

229

More important, he now realized, how could he possibly convince the boy of a lesson that in his heart he didn't believe in?

Graham drove on steadily. He turned left in the village and presently came out on to the main road that led to London and to his celebration dinner with Cole.